DISASTER IN THE NIGHT

Halliday fell into a heavy, dreamless sleep after daylight had grayed the window. It seemed to him that he was awakened again almost at once, by a pounding on the door. His fingers searched for the gun.

"Who is it?"

"Cap. Open up."

"What's the matter?"

"There's hell to pay. They stampeded the herd last night."

Norton charged in, shaking with anger.

"They hit us just after midnight. None of us expected trouble, and the two nighthawk riders didn't know what was happening until the first shots went off."

Halliday said: "Settle down. How many riders?"

"How in hell do I know? It was dark and the damn' cattle came charging right through our camp. A steer stepped on my chest. The wagon's gone. The camp's wrecked. And those doggies are scattered from hell to breakfast. I rode out with Gabe at first light. They did a real good job. Our stock is so mixed with Gunlock beef that it would take a full roundup to cut them out. When are María's Mexicans going to show up? The only way we'll get our herd back is to take over the whole ranch."

HIGH DESERT

TODHUNTER BALLARD

LEISURE BOOKS NEW YORK CITY

A LEISURE BOOK®

October 2005

Published by special arrangement with Golden West Literary Agency.

Dorchester Publishing Co., Inc.
200 Madison Avenue
New York, NY 10016

ISBN 0-8439-5618-6

The name "Leisure Books" and the stylized "L" with design are trademarks of Dorchester Publishing Co., Inc.

Printed in the United States of America.

Visit us on the web at www.dorchesterpub.com.

TABLE OF CONTENTS

Drifter's Choice

Wade Pierce locked the bank doors, descended the two worn steps, and turned along the sun-rotted wooden sidewalk of Front Street. To his restless eyes the broken boards represented the decay of the once flourishing town. This walk had been trod by many feet—boots that sprouted large-roweled Mexican spurs, cracked, worn from months on the dry trails from the south, gamblers' shoes, and the slippers of dancing girls.

Bullhorn had boomed as a trail town, the end of steel, where bellowing longhorns of the Bend country had met the boxcars that would take them East to slaughter. But like Baxter Springs and Wichita it had faded, joining the necklace of shipping points outmoded as the rails pushed West.

Its moment of glory was short lived as the railroad moved onward. The shipping pens remained, but now only a few thousand head of local stock filtered through the loading chutes each year, and it had become another cow town, settling into the pattern of slow change that had spread across the endless plains.

Only three saloons remained, sleepy in midweek inactivity, and what had been the biggest dance hall in the West now housed Horn's Emporium and Mercantile Establishment.

Pierce passed the store windows already lighted by their hanging lamps, and moved on to White's saloon, walking awkwardly, unaccustomed to the low-heeled shoes.

Two hours, he thought. *I've been home two hours and I wish I'd never come.* He paused before the swinging doors and looked bitterly at the dusty street.

A yellow dog, flea-bitten and nondescript, slunk from the livery barn to wallow in the deep powdered dirt. Old Mitchell closed the post office and walked with stiffened knees toward the yellow station, carrying a limp mail sack across his age-bent shoulders. Nothing else moved but the flies pestering the two discouraged ponies at the battered hitching rack. And old Mrs. Calhoun who rocked ceaselessly on her sway-backed porch.

Wade Pierce turned away, shutting the scene out of his mind, and entered the saloon. He felt uncomfortable in the neat black suit, the white shirt. The gun belt across his narrow hips seemed out of place, but without it he would have been entirely lost. Six years of badlands riding had made habit strong. There, survival had depended on watchfulness, and quickness of hand. This same habit made him sweep the long empty room with careful eyes. Only one swinging lamp burned, casting its amber glow in softening tinge alike on the scarred bar, the row of bottles against the expensive mirror, and the covered tables at the rear.

Ed White was behind his own bar, a spare man, his unbuttoned vest held together by a heavy watch chain. Six years ago Ed had had three bartenders working day and night. Then he had run the town from his office at the rear of the saloon, hiring fighting marshals, handing down orders with the ruthless impartiality of a just dictator. He still ran the town, still was mayor, but now he had time to tend his bar and doze each morning in a tilted chair on the saloon's gallery.

14

He looked up, creasing the weekly paper into a long triangle with which he swatted at the buzzing flies. "How's it seem to be the head of the bank?"

Wade Pierce came against the bar, one foot raised, the heel of his shoe hooked upon the rail. He inspected his image in the mirror without pleasure. "I look like a dressed-up drummer. I should be peddling whiskey or calico." His wide, slightly humorous mouth split a face drawn thin and tight by hard riding. His eyes against the sun-darkened skin were startlingly blue. His hair beneath the hat line had bleached yellow brown. It was darker on top, but still carried a touch of tow-headedness.

"You don't cut a bad face," said Ed White. "I'll venture you had them Montana girls crazy at Saturday dances. Your uncle was a stepper in his younger days."

"And a banker when I grew up." Wade Pierce accepted the bottle placed before him. He poured his drink and put it down with a single motion of his hand. "Why'd you send for me? I'm no banker. I never had five dollars from one pay to the next. Money in chunks scares me."

The man behind the bar shrugged. He used a cloth to mop up an imaginary spot, taking his time. "Someone had to carry on. You're the only Pierce left."

"Sure," said Pierce bitterly. "And no credit to the name, to use my uncle's words. He called me a saddle tramp, and he was right. There's something about forking a horse, climbing the next hill, just to see what she looks like on the far slope."

White moved his head slowly. "I know what you mean. I came up the Texas trail. But a man roots down and his ideas change. Someone has to run the bank."

"You run it," said Pierce. "I'll give it to you, free and clear. I want nothing but a horse to ride. Why should I be fenced into a money corral because I had an uncle who chose to start a bank?"

White leaned across the bar. "Don't think I'm crazy when I tell you that a fight is shaping up here. It's a bigger fight than most realize. It will take a young man, a strong man to lead."

Pierce's eyes narrowed. "Who wants to fight for a broken town in the middle of a thousand miles of prairie? You're dreaming, Ed, dreaming of the old trail days."

"No," said White, and his voice trembled. "Things are happening, Wade, happening all over the West. This is a small bank, serving a single valley, but it's a mirror of other banks in other valleys. After the war, the West was poor, starved, and no one offered us help. That was in the 'Seventies, and we had to drive our cows two thousand miles, but a change has come. Your uncle saw the change. It was he who understood, he who started toward the fight."

Pierce did not understand, but the strength of the old man's feeling shook him. "What's this about? The valley's all settled up, a section, maybe two apiece. What's there to fight about? What's there to fight for?"

White took time to answer, to arrange his words. "The land is settled up, yes, each man with his little part. That's why they came here, for land they could own, for a place to run their cows, to have feeder lots where they could fatten other stock. They buy and sell and they need cash to operate. It's these men who have made the land safe. But now, the grab is on. This is the 'Eighties and the East has discovered us. The banking interests are moving in. All over the West, the story is the same, vested capital, fighting the people for the land. In California, they tell me, the railroad is swallowing up the state. Here it's the banking crowd, using every weapon that they hold, grabbing individual banks, calling their loans, driving the people from the ownership of the land, making them into tenants as they were in the East."

"You're crazy," said Pierce. "I can show you a million acres to the north, still unfenced, still free range."

"In the north, yes!" Excitement had heightened White's tone. "The land hogs haven't reached there yet. But in this state they hold the upper hand. So far no one's stood against them, but your uncle. The other small banks watched his fight. They're still watching Bullhorn Valley. If we beat Sam Leavitt, they'll close ranks. If we lose, they'll sell out from sheer hopelessness."

Pierce's attention quickened. "Sam Leavitt, not the land boomer we used to laugh at with his immigrants?"

"The same," said the old man. "But few laugh at Sam now. He heads this new state bank with offices in the capital. His operations already cover twenty counties, and he wants this bank. He knows that it has become a kind of rallying point for all who dare to fight him. He'll try to buy you out. If he fails, he'll turn to other means. He can't brook opposition."

The import still failed to reach Wade Pierce. He was a riding man, not a banker. He couldn't foresee that this was the beginning of the struggle for control of the West, a struggle between lone men and giant interests, a struggle that caused one of the great land booms of history, and that would not end until the disastrous depression of 1893 would wipe out the inflated values. But he sensed that White's words came from a deeper concern than any personal consideration.

"Don't decide now, Wade. Sleep on it. Don't make any decision until morning."

Wade Pierce had a knowing eye for pretty women, but, the next morning, the girl in his uncle's office amazed him. He lounged just inside the door considering her as she bent above the old-fashioned roll-top desk, totally unconscious of his presence.

"Well," he said. "I'm not up on all the rules of banking, but I never heard that bank robbers were so pretty."

She spun with a surprised cry. Her fair hair was caught in a soft knot at the nape of her neck, but as she turned, one lock escaped to fall across her eyes. She brushed it back impatiently. "You must be Wade Pierce."

"I must be." He came forward, grinning.

"I'm Mary Colston." She said it as if she thought the name self-explanatory.

He bobbed his head. "Pleased to meet you, Mary Colston, but I still want to know, are you a bank robber?"

Her eyes widened and a spot of color came up into each rounded cheek. "That's not funny. You know I was your uncle's assistant."

"Well," said Pierce, and his smile widened, "there's a lot of nice things about banking they forgot to tell me. No wonder my uncle liked it."

Her flush turned to one of anger, and she said sharply: "I'll be very glad to resign, now that you've come."

He advanced until he stood directly in front of her. She was tall for a woman, but he was much taller, towering above her. "That would be a mistake, Mary. You know a lot more about this business than I do. You stay, I'll go back where I came from."

She was still angry. "Running away already?"

By instinct his big hands came up and gripped her shoulders. "No one ever accused me of running from anything, sweetheart." His eyes darkened and the smile was gone from the wide mouth.

She shook herself free. "Don't ever touch me again. Don't call me that." Her anger was like a flame. He had seen other women in a rage, but he had never seen one so self-possessed. "They called you wild, they said you had no stability."

"Who called me that?"

"The Evans family in Montana. That's how Ed White found you. They said you would ride a hundred miles for a joke, but were not one to keep a job."

His mouth twisted wryly. "I'm not used to people passing their judgments on my actions."

"A free soul," she was mocking him. "A forty-dollar horse and a fifty-dollar saddle. I know the kind. Your uncle used to talk about you. He deserved a better heir. He gave his life for this valley and now everything he worked for falls apart because there's no one to carry on. Doesn't it matter to you that Sam Leavitt's gang will gobble up the state, that men you knew, you grew up with, will be turned from their homes?"

"You sound like Ed White."

"Why not? Ed and I see the danger. Your uncle made us

understand, but we are almost alone. Not all the members of the bank board agree. Some of the merchants, Horn for instance, are working with Leavitt. Without you, without your stock behind us, they will win."

"I'll give it to you. I've already offered it to White."

Her anger increased. "Very funny, Mister Pierce. Let Leavitt win here and his power will increase a thousandfold. But why should you care that all of us will bow to his machine or leave the state? The men who came here that they might own land and be beholden to no one . . . you'll sell them to Leavitt because you're too heedless, too selfish. You wear a gun and people say you can use it. But it takes another kind of courage in this fight . . . and obviously you lack that kind."

Pierce said solemnly: "You don't need me. You're doing fine all by yourself. I'd as soon stand against you as a keg of dynamite, and, if Sam Leavitt can whip you, he's a better man than I think."

The girl choked as if anger halted further words. She turned then, and swept past him and from the room, jarring the glass panel as she slammed the door.

Pierce sat down at his uncle's desk. He was smiling to himself.

It was nearly eleven when old Dustin, the combination bookkeeper and clerk, appeared to say that Sam Leavitt was there.

The state bank man was big, dressed like a prosperous rancher. Only the softness of his hands showed that he was no outdoor man. He greeted Pierce as an old friend, his voice booming in the confines of the room. "Like old times to see you, Wade. Town's changed some in six years, not the wild place it was."

Pierce's mouth tightened. He had never cared for the ex–land agent, but he motioned his visitor to a chair and watched Leavitt sit down, finding irritation in the man's manner. There was an air of proprietorship as if Leavitt already felt himself the owner of this bank.

"Sad thing, your uncle's death," he boomed. "Always liked Henry, but death comes to us all."

Pierce's tone was short. "Let's not pretend grief, Sam. I hadn't seen him in six years, and, as you know, we did not get along."

The big man was surprised. He was a person who observed the outward polite niceties of life. But he recovered his poise as he mopped his red face with a handkerchief. "Which brings me to business then. This town is dead, done for. She never lived up to the dreams we all had when steel first came in from the East. But I've got a bank in the capital. We're standardizing the finances of the state. The best way is one big bank, working for everyone."

Pierce did not trouble to mask his dislike.

"And you," said Leavitt. "You're a range man, Wade. You're more comfortable on a horse than in a chair. You don't want to be troubled with the petty details of a bank."

He's using the same argument I gave Ed White and the girl, Wade thought. *I should agree. I should be pleased he wants to buy me out.* But a natural stubborn streak rose up. Aloud, he said: "I never meant to be a banker, and it was a surprise to be mentioned in my uncle's will."

"Every man to his own last," Leavitt beamed. "I won't beat around the bush. This institution is capitalized for one hundred thousand, a third of the stock is yours. I offer thirty-five thousand for it now, although, with conditions as they are, it's hardly worth face value."

"I don't know," said Pierce, for this was a game he understood, a game he'd played at many poker tables. "I hadn't thought of selling."

"Think of it now." Leavitt leaned forward eagerly. "Things are cheap, Wade. Thirty-five thousand will buy the best range in all Montana, if you choose to return."

That was right. Pierce doubted if there was that much hard cash in all the northern ranges. And he knew the place, where Cabin Creek came rushing out of the hills. A brand of his own. The picture built up in his mind. He found it pleasant to contemplate.

"You've got to think of yourself," said the big man. He tapped Pierce's knee. "I know Ed White called you home, but Ed's thinking in the past. He's standing against the best interests of the country."

The words jarred Pierce. White had always thought of the town first, and the valley. Leavitt had taken the wrong track, said the wrong thing, and Pierce was surprised by his own words. "I'm not selling, Sam. I guess I'm here to stay."

The genial mask slipped from Leavitt's face, leaving it hard and bleak, and his voice no longer boomed. "You're making a mistake, Wade. We'll crush you."

Pierce frowned at the threat. "I'm still not selling."

Leavitt rose, sensing the futility of argument. "You're ill-advised. You've been listening to Ed and the girl. They're using you for their own ends . . . they're making you into a fool."

Pierce came to his feet, his coat falling back, and the big man saw the gun belt at the narrow hips. The words died on his thick lips and he retreated quickly to the door.

It was the first board meeting Wade Pierce had ever attended, and he was glad to have Mary Colston there, although she still held her anger and offered him no greeting.

Leavitt appeared, but Leavitt was not alone. Pierce's eyes tightened as he recognized the lean sunburned man who followed the banker in.

Monk Moore belonged to an earlier day. A cowboy once, then a railroad detective, he had blazed his name across the West. Now he was Leavitt's field agent, cold and watchful.

Backed by Moore, Leavitt swaggered as he took his seat. Behind him came the others, Ed White, old and uncomfortable in his rusty business suit. Dutch Harmony, the solid, slow-moving rancher from Grass Creek, and Robert Horn who ran the big store.

This, then, was the board. Leavitt sat here because he had already bought up small holdings until he owned a fourth of the bank's stock. But it was Horn who opened the meeting. Pierce had never liked the merchant. As a boy he had delighted in riding past the store's loading platform, roping and dragging off any merchandise left outside.

He listened now as the storekeeper spoke, his voice dry and emotionless. "As long as Henry Pierce lived," Horn said, "I supported the interests in this bank who strove to keep outsiders from coming in. But Henry's dead, and none is trained to take his place." He turned and looked at Pierce, and old hate showed in his dark eyes. There was a relationship between these two that few men guessed, something buried for six years that colored judgment now. He went on, and his voice had not changed. "I feel our whole position is unsound." He explained in detail then, the number of notes overdue, interest payments that had not been made.

Wade Pierce lost the thread of the words. He thought: *Horn still hates me because of Judith. He's sold out because it is a way to strike at me. And he's the leader of the merchants as he always was. He'll carry them all into Leavitt's camp.* He turned a little in his creaking chair and put his full attention on Dutch Harmony.

The rancher's solid face had not changed expression. It was impossible to guess his thoughts. Pierce knew that Harmony and his ranchers held the balance of the power. On one side lined up Leavitt and the Horn interests, on the other White, the girl, and himself. It remained for the ranchers to decide. If Harmony voted against him, all was lost.

Robert Horn knew this, too. He appealed directly to the man. "The good of the whole valley rests with this bank. We can't afford to shut ourselves off from the whole of the state, and that is exactly what we'll do if we refuse Leavitt's offer. Alone, we certainly can't beat this state group, therefore, I say, in self protection, Bullhorn had best join them."

He sat down, his appeal finished, and Harmony had the floor. He spoke carefully, examining each word.

"Every ranch in the valley is mortgaged to this bank. No ranch has anything but cattle with which to pay. Personally I'd rather owe money in Bullhorn than in the capital. I'd rather deal with neighbors than Eastern men." He settled back, and Leavitt rose.

"You forget I'm a local man," he said. "You forget the interests of this valley are close to my heart. I can save you all if you give me the chance, but I warn you now that, if you fail to join us, we'll have to fight you."

Mary Colston was on her feet. "You'll help us?" she demanded with dead earnestness. "You'll help us as you helped people of Buffalo Creek. You bought their bank and called its loans. Who owns the valley now? I'll tell you who, a cattle company, financed in the East, run by hired hands for stockholders who live two thousand miles away. We don't want that in this valley. That isn't the reason men

24

lived through their first year, buried deep in sod houses to escape the winter cold. If we sell them out, their voices will ring like thunder to shout us down. We will have lost our homes, our self-respect. I'd beg or steal or cheat to stop you, Sam Leavitt. I almost think I'd kill." Her eyes swept the circle of silent men. Then she was gone, running blindly out of the room.

Leavitt laughed, the booming sound bringing them out of their spell. "That's why women have no place in business," he said. "They get too emotional. Mary means the best in the world, but certainly we can't afford to trust our bank to the management of a woman and a saddle tramp who by all accounts has spent six years carrying a straight iron."

Wade Pierce stirred. A straight iron was used to change a brand. It was a studied insult to provoke a fight. He watched not Leavitt, but Monk Moore, knowing that the danger lay in this quiet man.

It was obvious now that Leavitt knew the fight here was lost, that he was turning to other things. It was a signal that Pierce could not ignore for death might well be the result. But he pretended not to hear. If it was a fight they wanted, he would give them one. But not in this crowded room. He sat silently and listened as they voted Leavitt down, knowing that, although the first round was won, the battle had hardly been engaged. That would come later.

III

Light from the hotel lobby laid a yellow pattern across the gallery and out into the street. Three drummers filled the cane-bottomed chairs and told their stories, their ready laughter riding out across the dark.

Wade heard their laughter as he left the bank. It gave him a sense of loneliness that he did not understand. He was used to long trails, to no company save his own thoughts. But here, in the center of a town, he felt alone, felt that he did not belong. He had spent the evening on the books, verifying what Horn had said about the condition of the bank. Even to his untutored eyes the situation seemed dangerous. Too much of the capital and deposits were tied up in loans on which not even the interest had been paid. He did not need anyone to tell him what would happen if all the depositors suddenly decided to withdraw their funds. There was less than $10,000 in cash on hand.

Wearily he turned toward his hotel room. He passed the Horn store and was surprised to hear a woman call his name from the dark entrance. He halted. Judith Horn came slowly out of the shadow to face him.

Seeing her was a shock. She stood against the background of light from Ed White's place, and one searching moment told him she was more beautiful than he remembered. This was the girl he had loved, the girl who had sent him riding northward on the long trail. She had the dark beauty of her Spanish mother, the full rich warmth of the southern races. He had squired her to her first dance, against her father's pleasure, had watched her grow, had watched her flirt with other men, and had stood by while she married Will Jarmane. He knew, standing there, that he would not have returned had he known she was still in town.

Her tone was as soft and caressing as the darkness. "You've been avoiding me, Wade."

"I didn't guess you were here. I supposed your husband had taken you East."

"Will's dead," she told him simply. "He died the spring after you left. You could have found out, had you cared."

He did not explain that he purposely sought no news of Bullhorn, that he had tried to forget the town. He stood there and the silence became strained until she spoke again.

"I want to talk to you if you have a little time."

He nodded. "I've nothing else to do."

She seemed not to notice his cool reply and led him up the steps at the side of the store building to the rooms where Horn lived.

Pierce paused in the doorway and looked around. Horn had prospered, but the rooms had not changed with the years. They were still ugly and uncomfortable. It was a place to flop in, rather than a home, and he could not wonder that Judith had fled to Jarmane's arms for warmth and love.

Will Jarmane had had taste and knowledge and understanding, for all he was a gambling man. He had been polished in a way that Pierce would never be. It was hardly a contest between them; it had not been a contest from the first time the gambler had smiled at the dark-haired girl.

Wade turned to look at her now. Against his hardened resolve he had to admit that the last few years had added to the fullness of her charms. And she was smiling the same provocative smile he remembered. And the dark eyes seemed to beg.

"Like me a little, Wade, just a little for old times' sake."

He spoke, finding his voice not steady: "I'm glad to see you, Judith. This is like old times. I begin to feel that maybe I've come home."

"Maybe you have, Wade." She motioned him toward a chair. "I was hurt at first, after Will's death, when you did not come, then I was hurt last night, when I heard you were in town, yet you made no effort to see me. It did not seem possible that you did not know I was here."

"I had no way of knowing."

"No," she told him. "I guess you had no way of knowing, but, although your apparent neglect hurt me, I pocketed my pride to talk to you tonight. I couldn't let you go unwarned."

He looked at her sharply. "Warned?"

"About the bank," she said.

"What about the bank?"

"The bank is gone." Her voice was low. "I overheard my father talking, and he's not one who makes mistakes where business is concerned."

Wade started to tell her that her father had sold out, but he held his words.

"Think of your position," she said. "When the bank fails, all the people will blame you for their lost savings. Why should you take that blame? For it will fail. You must stop listening to White and that Colston girl. They'll ruin you. Sell while you can before they strike you. Take your money, buy your Montana ranch, leave Bullhorn to its own troubles."

She leaned forward as she talked. Her eyes were warm and intimate, holding out an unspoken promise and he thought: *She's right, of course. This isn't my fight. I can have my ranch and, unless I misread the signs, take her north with me.* And then he thought of Sam Leavitt. His face hardened. "No, Judith."

The warmth died from her face, leaving it strained. "You've listened to Mary Colston and her speeches. She's sold you on something, perhaps on herself. You're different, Wade, you're not the boy I knew. You're stupid and stubborn and bull-headed. Go your way. Get yourself killed, but, when the time comes, only remember that I tried to warn you and that it was not me, but Mary Colston, who got you into this."

He stared at her, not understanding. He started to tell her that she was wrong, that he had not been thinking of the Colston girl at all. And then he closed his lips and rose. What was the use of further argument?

The hotel room was hot and close. He opened the single window and stood smoking, looking off across the roofs of the darkened town. His window faced the back, and he could not see Front Street from where he stood. Beneath the window ran the slanting roof of the rear gallery, beyond it a trampled yard and ancient barn. His eyes were on the clustered roofs, but his mind considered other things.

Mary Colston had made her speech at the bank. He hadn't seen her since, but the angry way she had faced Leavitt made pleasant remembrance. Certainly she had hoped for nothing by her stand. It was an honest gesture brought forth by impulsive rage. A firebrand in a simple dress. But Judith's motives were not entirely clear. What had she hoped for? What had she wished to gain? Certainly she must have known that any time during the past years a word from her would have brought him back down the trail. But she had never sent that word, and yet tonight she had sought him out. He could not understand women's minds. He ground out his cigarette upon the sill and turned to bed.

He slept, as he always slept, with ears alert. He heard the drummers mount the stairs and make the noisy passage to their rooms. The house settled. A lone horse went out of town at a half run. A dog yelped from the direction of the livery corral, and far off a swelling chorus of coyotes answered him.

Suddenly Pierce was wide-awake. He lay still, listening. The room and hall beyond were blanketed in darkness. Only the pale rectangle of the window enabled him to orient himself.

The noise came again, men's voices from outside.

He rose, his feet soundless on the old boards, and reached the window. A rind of moon showed above the warped stable and shone faintly on half a dozen men. He watched them, studying each carefully. He recognized the leader. Monk Moore waited beside his horse, giving low-voiced orders to the crowd. *This was Leavitt's answer,* thought Wade. Violence was to take the place of argument. This was what Judith Horn had tried to tell him.

He turned swiftly in the darkness and found his pants and boots. The gun belt sagging across his hips restored his confidence. He lifted the heavy weapon and held it lightly in his hand, then moved to the open doorway as he heard the shuffling on the stairs.

They came along the hall, two men, feeling their way.

Pierce's lips curved grimly in the darkness, then he heard the muttered: "Hell, the door's open. Something's wrong."

The whispered answer was sharp and distinct. "What's wrong? It's hot. He left it open for air. Go on."

They moved into the room. Pierce could smell the sweat of their riding clothes, the hotness of their bodies. He struck as the second man's outline moved between him and the window light, feeling the jar as the heavy barrel buffaloed the head.

The one in advance turned, bringing up his gun, but he was too late. Pierce's arm chopped down a second time, the metal crashing dully against bone.

The relief of action flowed through him as a tonic. He laughed quietly to himself and stepped across the twisted bodies to the window. His impulse was to step out on the gallery roof, to leap lightly to the ground and face Monk Moore down, bringing this whole struggle to a head. But common sense told him that was not the way. Leavitt was not here and Sam would carry on no matter what happened to Moore and the men in the yard below.

He had to slip from the hotel. The thought of running was contrary to all his impulses, but he wasted no time. He ran downstairs, stepped quickly from the doorway toward the livery.

The challenge from behind him cut the still night. "That you, Joe?"

The gun in Pierce's hand sent a bellowing explosion in the gloom. A man's cry blended upward with the echoes of the shot. Behind the hotel shouts rose. Pierce splintered the hotel's corner with a second bullet, turned, and ran. No hope to reach the livery now. No hope of gaining his horse. He cut across Front Street and sprinted between two buildings, vaulting a low fence.

Memory came back to guide him. As a boy he had played among these same buildings. He knew every alley, every twist and path. Once this had been the district housing cheap saloons and dance halls. Beyond was the railroad with its loading pens, the switching yard, guarded by the water tower. Now the buildings housed Mexicans and poor whites, or stood empty and gaping.

He moved again, more slowly now, keeping close to the building line until he reached the railroad. Behind him the town came to life. Half a hundred houses showed lights. Men moved grimly, hunting him like an animal. He knew they had fanned out, making a line along Front Street so that he could not double back to the residential side.

There was little time to think and none to waste. He heard the low whistle of the freight, its puffing engine struggling with the long drag as it fought the slight grade from the west. He jumped across the tracks and dropped, belly-flat, in the sheltering weeds. The engine came on, its flickering light washing across the station and the yards. He caught the irons of the fourth car and, swinging up, climbed to the top.

From this vantage point he watched the lights of the town fade. Then he put it from his mind and considered what to do. It was three hours to the capital, but there were other stations in between, other towns in which he might sleep safely.

IV

The noon train, crowded with westward immigrants, pulled into Bullhorn twenty-five minutes late. The engine man called his greeting to the stationmaster and swung down with his long-snouted oilcan.

Wade Pierce stepped from the last car. He had dropped off the freight at Buffalo Creek and spent the night on a hard station bench. He left the train on the side away from the platform. He rounded the train and walked across one corner of the wooden platform.

The usual crowd of town people was missing, but the few who loitered in the shade of the overhang put their full attention upon him. He gave them a searching look, found no danger here, and stepped across the switch track to enter Railroad Avenue. Ahead of him was the town's main intersection with the bank standing to the right. He saw the crowd about the entrance, a swelling half circle that spread across the sidewalk and into the street. Then he went on, lengthening his steps, and came across the fringes of the crowd.

Men turned under his hands, their faces changing and showing bewilderment. Someone called: "He's here! He's come back!" And the crowd split so that he made the pas-

33

sage to the door of the bank. Inside, the pack pushed toward the single wicket behind which old Dustin paid out money. Several reached to catch his arm, shouting their demands or waving their open passbooks beneath his nose. He used his shoulders to push them aside, and somehow gained the office door and slid through. Then he put the bolt in place and turned around.

White and the girl had swung to face him.

"We thought you'd gone," said White. His voice was tired; his shoulders sagged.

Wade looked at the girl. "Did you think so, too? Did you think I'd run away?"

She sat down, weary from the tension. "I didn't know what to think. I don't know that you'd be blamed for running out. There isn't anything left that we can do. If you'd been here this morning, when it first started, we might have checked it. But Leavitt's men have spread across the town. They've whispered that the bank's not safe, that you took funds last night and disappeared."

"But I'm here now. Those fools saw me come in."

She shook her head, and it hurt him to watch her giving up.

He said firmly: "I don't know much about these things, but I can't see where we're whipped yet. True, we haven't the cash on hand to pay all the depositors, but we have assets, notes on loans. Can't we explain that to the people? Can't we show them the books?"

White shook his head. "Those people out there aren't thinking quickly. They're scared. They only know they want their money, and they're afraid that it is gone. When we've paid out the last cash, we close the doors, and then the banking commissioner steps in. He'll appoint a receiver, and Leavitt controls the commission. They'll call the loans, and force the mortgage payments. Those who can't pay will be closed out."

"Explain that to the depositors."

"No use," said White. "They'd howl me down. Did you ever try and argue with a scared man? He's more dangerous than all the heroes ever born. You'll be held responsible for this, and none of it is your fault. They'll probably try and lynch you after the doors close."

"Mary," said Pierce, forcing her to look up at him. "You know more about this business than I do. Start thinking. There must be something we can do. Can't we raise money from other banks on our loans?"

She shook her head. "Our correspondent is Leavitt's state bank. It's run by Ralph Forbes in the capital. Naturally we can't expect help from him. As for the others, the small banks like ourselves, they know that, as soon as we're whipped, Leavitt will turn on them. They don't dare to move for fear of increasing his wrath."

"But if we whipped him?"

"Whip him first, then you'll have all the help you need. It's always that way, Wade. People will follow a leader, after he's winning." He stared at her helplessly. She rose and laid a hand on his arm. "Ed's right. We got you into this. It was a hopeless fight already. You've got to get out of town. I'm sorry about the things I said yesterday. I didn't mean them, and I don't want you hurt. It's the last thing I want . . . for you to be hurt."

He took both her hands. "Listen to me, Mary. We're not through yet. There was ten thousand cash this morning. It takes time to pay that out in small amounts. Tell Dustin to take all the time he can. Tell him to keep paying until closing, then shut the doors. Time's on our side. Somehow, somewhere, I'll find help by morning."

He saw by her face that she did not believe him. He saw that Ed White did not believe him, either. They both thought he was running away. Well, let them. He went out through the rear door. He had no clear plan, nothing except he meant to find Leavitt and force the big man to save the bank.

He moved along the alley and passed behind Horn's store, and from the rear door Judith again called his name. His first impulse was to ignore her, but after an instant's hesitation he turned and crossed the loading platform and stepped inside.

"Wade," she said, and caught his arm as he stepped in. "What happened to you? How'd you escape?"

"I rode out on the train."

"The orders were that you would be captured, but only held out of town until the bank was closed. You're caught in this bank failure and you will be blamed."

"Will that matter to you?" he asked, and realized that the words were merely automatic, that he no longer cared.

She was as desirable as ever, but somehow, somewhere he had changed. For six years he had nursed memory, seeing her image in every campfire that he built, but now that she stood before him, the memory became unreal, a dream that failed in its fulfillment even when she told him: "You know it matters, Wade. It always did, although I had to marry someone else to find it out. When Will died, I thought it was too late. But you're back now and I am here to save you. I can get the money that you need to pay the depositors."

"You can?"

She nodded quickly, eagerly. "Yes, you can pay them off and then make your deal with Sam. I know how such things are done. I'll draw a check against your bank. With my father's credit behind you, there will be no difficulty. Anyone will cash it in Kansas City or Saint Louis. It will take three days for the check to clear the clearinghouse. By that time you will have stopped the run, and once people learn that they can get their money, they will start redepositing. You'll have the money to pay my check when it comes from the clearinghouse. It's a way of getting credit without asking for it."

He looked at her. "That doesn't sound too honest."

She laughed at him. "You never change, do you, Wade? There is a difference between sharp business practice and dishonesty. I'll help you, Wade, but first you must make a deal with me. When the bank is saved, you'll sell out to my father and to Sam. We'll take the money and leave Bullhorn."

He frowned. "But that's what I could have done yesterday had I been willing to sell out the valley to Leavitt's crowd. The small ranchers still look to me for help."

She flashed at him. "You ask too much. I offer you a chance to save your neck and you talk about the valley. Is it the valley that holds your interest, or that Colston girl?"

He looked at her and laughed. It was the first real laugh he'd had that day. "You're smart," he said. "I guess you always were too smart for me, Judith. I see that now. You read my mind when I can't read it myself."

She flushed and her eyes were angry dark. "You're a fool," she told him savagely. "All bets are off. See if it helps the valley and the girl when those angry depositors hang you to the water tower." She turned and moved away.

He watched her for a minute, then he left the store.

The station lay deserted in the afternoon heat. The whole town's interest still centered at the bank. The telegraph operator sat before his clattering relay, penciling invoices of freight. He did not turn until Pierce shoved the message beneath the grill and called. The operator was not a local man. He read the message aloud without interest.

Ralph Forbes
State Banking Company
   Please extend every courtesy to Wade Pierce. He is now one of us.

Leavitt

He made the count and gave Pierce his change, then turned to the key and started sending.

Up at the head of Railroad Avenue, Pierce could still see the crowd about the bank. Even as he heard the whistle of the train, he saw White appear, herding the crowd before him, and lock the building's doors. For an instant Wade Pierce knew the bitter hopelessness of defeat, then glanced at his watch and saw it was after three. Another banking day had passed and he had until morning to raise some funds.

He was the first one on the train when it came in, and his impatience grew as it failed to move. If someone from the crowd had spotted him, they might prevent his leaving town. But no one came and the train rolled at last.

The capital had changed. He remembered it as a raw country town. There was a state house now, a new station, and six blocks of business houses and stores.

He went first to the Western Hotel, washed and cleaned himself. Then he sought Forbes. It was long after hours and he found the banker at his residence.

Forbes shook hands, insisting that Pierce join them for dinner. "I got Sam's wire," he said. "I'm glad to see that you've joined us, that the possibility of trouble is past. We tried to convince your uncle, but he could not see that his best interests lay with us."

Pierce nodded. This was like a game. Pierce told him: "I hate to ask this, knowing it is after hours. But I'm heading north now that you're taking over my interests. I have a little deal in cattle to close first, and the seller, being an old-timer, insists on gold."

The whole thing was so easy that it scared him. Forbes went to get his hat, and together they moved down to the bank. Requests for cash in cattle purchases were still a standard procedure here. Pierce gave him a check drawn on the Bullhorn bank. It amused him as he wrote his sprawling signature. He watched the banker count out the gold. He thanked the man.

"We're all together on this," Forbes said. "We'll all make our fortunes in this state. A solid man, Sam Leavitt, and one it pays to tie to."

"So I've found," said Pierce. "Tell Sam how I appreciate his help." They separated on the walk before the bank, and Pierce turned quickly to the station, the fifty odd pounds in the bag bumping against his leg. His right hand was free, close to the belted gun. The game was almost in his hands, but he found that it would be a good two hours before the train would come.

The sun was dropping from sight when he reached his hotel room. He drew a chair forward and sat down, watching the empty street below. The gong sounded from the dining room, but he did not stir although he had not eaten since morning. There was a rising tide of excitement within him, a nervousness entirely foreign to his nature.

He thought: *I'm jumpy as a cat. I wasn't cut out to be a thief. I'll get this money back to Bullhorn and light out. Ed can see the check is paid when things quiet down.* He glanced at his watch and was surprised to see that barely five minutes had passed. He built a cigarette and smoked slowly, feeling the bag with the toe of his shoe. *This is silly,* he thought. *There's no reason for Forbes to guess that anything is wrong.*

Then he stiffened. Forbes was hurrying across the street. He was not alone. The bulky man at his side almost ran to keep up. Light flicked on the badge pinned to his shirt.

Pierce picked up the gold and ran into the hall. There was a stairway at the rear. He used this to gain the area behind the long, frame building. Darkness was heavy here, and he crossed quickly to the dust-cushioned alley, and along it to the side street. The hunt was on.

He must catch the evening train. But the station was the first place they would watch. It would be the focal point of the hunt. He moved along the street away from the business district. He reached the dead end and stepped over the wire fence, crossing the field beyond, thanking the luck that made the moon obscure.

It seemed he covered miles, skirting the town's edge until he reached the single line of rails. Out of the night loomed the water tower. He plodded toward the tank, seeing the station lights well beyond.

The bag jarred heavily against his leg, its contents giving small clicking sounds as he walked. He came to a stop between the tower and the station. He settled down until his shoulders were hidden by the growth.

The train was due. He saw travelers gathered in small knots on the distant platform. Among them moved several men. These he guessed were looking for him and he smiled grimly through the screen of weeds.

The whistle of the train. He watched far down the track where the headlamp would appear and saw it approach, like a Cyclops giant peering at the night. It paused a good five minutes at the platform. Then it moved on up to the tank, and he heard the gush of water released through the hose.

Not until the drivers spun did he move. Like a shadow he came out of the weeds to grasp the iron at the front of the baggage coach. The increasing speed of the train swung him up, his feet finding the lowest step, then he climbed, crawling out onto the car's convex top and lying there, belly-flat against the wind.

Hot cinders poured from the unscreened stack. They burned his cheeks and neck. He clung there, swearing for an hour, twice forced to beat out sparks that tried to burn his clothes. *To hell with this,* he thought, and scrambled, crab-like, along the car until he reached the other end. Here he lowered himself on the ladder to the open platform of the first coach and took a minute examining the occupants through the glass door.

Most of the passengers slept. The first seat was empty and he thrust the door inward as quietly as possible and stepped from the swaying platform, and seated himself. No one seemed to pay him any attention. He put the bag between his feet and settled, pulling down his hat brim to shadow his face. He sat motionless, staring through the small square window that showed the end of the lurching baggage coach. The train rattled and jerked over its uneven roadbed. A slightly flat wheel hammered. The air was close and hot, and gradually his senses dulled, relaxed by the absence of any danger.

Fresh sound brought him fully awake. He turned to see that the door at the back of the car had been pushed inward and two men were entering. A sharp glance showed that he had seen neither before, but he trusted only one quick look, then faced the front and watched their progress in the small

41

square window. Its coated dirt increased the mirror effect and he saw clearly how they paused to examine each passenger. He shifted a little to free his gun. Then he sat quietly, waiting.

As they reached the side of Pierce's seat, he turned his face, and brought the gun into sight. Both men were motionless, hampered by the confines of the aisle. "Don't move. Face the other side." He lifted their guns. "Now open the door."

His voice had been so low pitched, their movements so unhurried, that not one of the sleepers had waked. "On the platform," he said, and, leaving their guns in the seat, followed them to the door.

They clung to the hand rails, blocked in further progress by the blind end of the baggage coach. The train was laboring up a grade.

"Jump," said Pierce.

"Hey," said the man that was tall and thin, his cheeks drawn in as if from lack of food. "We'll kill ourselves."

"Not in those weeds." Pierce was inflexible. "Roll when you land, but jump."

"The devil with you!"

"Jump or I'll shoot you off."

The thin-faced man looked at him, then at the gun. He went slowly down the steps, stood for an instant, looking back, then, turning, yanked his hat tightly on his head and disappeared into the night.

The second man licked dry lips. His eyes sought Pierce's face as if searching for some sign of relenting. He found none. With a shrug he went down the three steps and leaped.

Pierce turned back to glance along the car. One or two sleepers stirred, muttering against their cramped positions, but none had awakened. He picked up the two guns, stepped back across the high sill, and threw them from the train. That done he closed the door and returned to his seat. It was still a long ride to Bullhorn, but he thought that now it should be undisturbed.

V

The first houses of Bullhorn raced past the window as the engine fought to slow the pushing cars.

Pierce lifted the bag and stepped outside, letting the sudden rush of fresh air clear his head of the stale fumes from the coach. Then he went down the steps on the far side and peered ahead, leaning out as far as he could to see the platform and the track ahead, bathed in the engine's light.

He had a fleeting, sweeping look at the platform, expecting it to be filled with Leavitt's men. It wasn't, and their absence puzzled him. He dropped off into the weeds before the train stopped and waited there, watching.

The stop was short, not over a couple of minutes. Above the line of his head the moving row of lighted windows blended as the train picked up momentum. Then it was gone, and he stood alone beyond the reach of the station lights, facing the platform across the right of way. The stationmaster turned his eyes from the fading lamps of the now speeding train. He set his signal arm for the eastbound freight, then moved inside the building and closed the door.

Pierce crossed the tracks, stepping up onto the planks of the walk. Still nothing happened. His lack of understanding increased as he rounded the corner and started up Railroad Avenue.

From the shadow of the feed store gallery a man stepped into view. Thirty feet separated them, and the light was on the hazy side, but Pierce knew as certainly as if it had been high noon that he faced Monk Moore. He stopped, motionless as a statue in a park, then called: "Where's your men, Monk?"

"No men," said Moore. "I never thought you'd get this far. And I need no help. Give me the gold."

"Come after it," Pierce said.

He saw Moore move, watchful as a coiling snake. Moore had moved half a dozen steps. But Pierce made no move. He stood as if rooted to the spot, the bag still hanging heavily from his left hand.

"Give me the gold," Monk repeated.

Pierce let mockery ride his tone. "I've got it, Monk. You take it away from me."

"I'll take it." Moore made his move. It was hard to see his hand, but he had crouched a little, and his was the first shot. Pierce was certain of that. He heard the man's bullet pass even as he swung up his own heavy barrel and fired. It seemed he, too, had missed. He fired again and again.

He saw Moore crumple. Pierce felt a sting in his leg. He took a step and found he still could walk. Monk Moore was dead. Pierce looked down at him without regret. He had no elation, no rancor. The man had played his game and lost. It was the way things were. He could not have walked onto the bank if Moore had lived. But he walked now, holstering his gun, conscious of a pain he hadn't felt before.

The shots had brought life to the town. He feared that they might bring Leavitt's men before he reached the bank. He hurried, hobbling along, wondering if he would have to

45

crawl the last 100 yards. He wasn't conscious of the blood he'd lost.

Ed White found him on the floor before the old safe. Ed had a scatter-gun in the crook of his arm. He took one look at the white face, the blood-soaked leg, then he was slicing the cloth away and fixing a tourniquet. He worked rapidly, his fingers sure. Then he spun to the bank door and sent a runner for the doctor.

The whole street was alive with people now, and Sam Leavitt came pushing through, the sheriff at his heels. Pierce was conscious of Leavitt's presence and managed a smile. The big man's face was a blotted red, uneven and spotty with almost a bluish tinge.

"Arrest him!" Leavitt told the sheriff. "He stole twenty thousand dollars from the bank in the capital. Where is it, Pierce?"

Pierce smiled. "You've got me, Leavitt." His voice was a little weak. "But the money is in that safe, and it belongs to this bank."

Leavitt was threatened with a stroke. It was all he could do to enunciate his words. "You can't get away with this. The courts. . . ."

"I have gotten away with it," said Pierce. "No one, not even the sheriff, can touch the money in this safe. And I didn't rob your bank, Sam. I cashed a check."

"A worthless check."

"How do you know? Has it been presented here for payment yet? Has that payment been refused? Wait until it is, then you will know whether you have a case or not." He passed out then.

The doctor looked and snorted once. "A clean hole," he said. "The bullet passed clear through. There's nothing wrong a good rest and a lot of food won't cure. He's lost a lot of blood, and how he ever walked in here without help, I'll never know."

They carried Pierce to the hotel, and put him to bed. Leavitt swore out a double warrant, for bank robbery and murder, but Pierce did not know. It was well into the afternoon before his mind was clear and the first person he saw beside the bed was White, sitting quietly, watchful as a mother hen.

"How goes it?" he said, and couldn't understand why he was so very weak.

White grunted. "Lie still and don't use up your strength. And don't let that deputy sitting in the hall worry you. As soon as Judge Cramer gets back, we'll have those fool warrants dismissed. No jury in this town would hold you responsible for killing Moore, not when the gun was still in his hand, with four shots gone and one of them in your leg. A thing like that needs no witnesses, not when Moore's reputation is well known."

"The bank," said Pierce, "what about it?"

"Forget the bank," said White. "Don't keep asking questions. You've lost a lot of blood. The bank's all right. I took the gold from the safe and had it heaped in sight on the counter when we opened this morning. It was remarkable how few wanted to withdraw their accounts when they saw that stack of double eagles shining at them. Confidence is a funny thing. You have it or you don't. It's not a matter of talk or reason, just a feeling each man must get himself."

Pierce relaxed and closed his eyes as White went on: "The story is all over town, how you whipped Leavitt at his own game. You're pretty close to a hero now, and only yesterday they would have gladly hung you to the nearest pole. But the telegraph operator talked. He told how you wired

47

Forbes in Leavitt's name, and then how Judith came and questioned him, and after her questions, the string of wires Leavitt sent."

Pierce opened his eyes. "So that's how they found out what I had done. It was Judith who gave me the idea in the first place."

Ed White's old eyes were shrewd. "Three times today she's come here to see you, but I wouldn't let her in. Judith's a woman, Wade, a pretty one, and dangerous."

Pierce smiled. "Stop worrying, Ed. She won't get around me again."

"I'm not so sure." White shook his old head. "A man like Leavitt is slippery, but you can back him down and then he'll quit. A woman like Judith never quits until she has her way, and sometimes not even then."

"Stop talking about Judith," Pierce said. "And tell me about Mary. Hasn't she been here? Hasn't she even asked how I was?"

"She hasn't had time," said White. "She's been the busiest person in this state."

Pierce's mouth was no longer humorous. "I suppose I could expect nothing more. Her first . . . her only thought . . . is for the bank. In a time like this she'd have no chance to worry about anything else."

White's mouth twitched at one corner, but his eyes were as solemn as an owl's. "That's right. She worries about banking constantly. Why, ever since last night when you were hurt, she's been doing nothing else but sending telegrams. I think she's wired every independent bank in the state. She's told each the full story of what you did, and told them that she needs to raise twenty thousand to meet the bad check you drew. You'd be surprised how persuasive that girl can be. On every train, by every stage, the money

48

has been pouring in. There's so much in our safe right now, I'm getting scared. I've hired an extra guard. We can meet your check now, a good ten times. I didn't know there was so much gold in the state."

Pierce tried to sit up, but White pushed him down. "Lie still, you fool. The whole country is celebrating. You don't want that celebration to end in your funeral, do you?"

"But where is she?"

"Why, in the hall. She's been there waiting this last half hour for you to come awake. But the doc said that you weren't to have excitement, and personally I'd say that Mary was exciting."

"Send her in, you old fool." Pierce closed his eyes, and, when he opened them, she was standing beside the bed, looking down at him.

"How are you, Wade?"

"I'm fine," he said. "I'm all but well. I've got to get out of here."

"You'll lie still," she told him, "until the doctor says you can get up. Don't be a dunce."

His mouth quirked. "It seems I was a dunce. It seems I caused a lot of trouble and killed a man, all to no purpose."

Her gray eyes clouded as she failed to understand. "All to no purpose, you say?"

"Why, yes. White's been telling me. He says you wired the small banks, and they've been sending money to help us out. Why didn't you do that yesterday? It would have been much simpler than all the hocus-pocus I went through."

"You don't understand," she told him, and sat down on the edge of the bed, taking his hand in both of hers. "I couldn't have made the appeal yesterday, and if I had, it wouldn't have done any good."

"You mean you did it to meet my check, to keep me

from going to prison for theft?"

She smiled a little. "Listen, Wade, there's nothing in this world I wouldn't do to help you in any way I could. But you've got to understand. Yesterday each small bank was scared of Leavitt. They were holding all their reserves, too frightened to offer help to us or anyone. Then you pulled your play. You beat Leavitt at his own game, and confidence and hope came alive. Yesterday I could merely wire an appeal. Today I offered all a chance to live, a chance to carry on. A chance to fight under your leadership."

"Not mine," he said, and grinned. "The idea was Judith Horn's. I'll admit that she did not plan the outcome quite as it worked, but, without her, I'd have never thought of it."

Mary said fiercely: "Listen to me, Wade Pierce. I've talked with Judith today. She had the nerve to come and see me at the bank. She told me how you'd loved her all your life. She warned me off because she considered you belonged to her. The way it's told in stories, people are supposed to play fair. You don't tear down your rivals . . . you sit by and let them practice all their underhanded tricks. Well, if those are the rules, I have no use for rules. I won't sit by and see her worm her way in here. I told White to keep her out. You're too good for her, Wade. I won't let her have a chance at you again."

He grinned and gripped her hand. "Tell me, am I too good for you?"

She said: "You're pretty certain of yourself, aren't you?"

His smile widened. "Your words are enough to turn any rider's head. You've been flattering me ever since I came. But if I can't have Judith, don't I get you?"

She tried to pull away. "You're laughing at me now."

Somewhere he found the strength to hold her tightly, and he was laughing. "Answer me."

"A girl's supposed to keep a man guessing. That's one of the rules."

"Make up your mind . . . you said you didn't play by rules."

"Stop laughing at me." She was getting angry. "You've got to be serious."

"Why? Leavitt's beaten."

"We've got to consolidate our gains, to keep the small banks linked for mutual protection, for the protection of everyone."

"Sweetheart, you make a pretty speech. I never thought I'd have a wife who talked like a Fourth of July orator."

"There, you're laughing at me again."

He was suddenly stern. "Look, honey, and this is as important as any fight. You take things too seriously. Relax a little. Learn to smile. Laugh at yourself and at what happens. Sometime that's the only saving grace. I'm not as smart as you, perhaps, but I know that laughter has its place, and there are other things."

She gave him a small smile. "I guess you're right."

"Certainly I'm right. Now kiss me so that I can see whether your kisses are as sweet as Judith's. That's important, too."

"You're mocking me again."

"No, just laughing with you. Some men have to kid about serious things."

She kissed him. "How was that?"

"I think maybe you'll learn," he said. "Try it again. I guess we'll have to stay and run the bank. If we went to a ranch, there'd be no one but the cattle to listen to your speeches."

"And maybe a good thing," she said, and this time it was she who laughed.

Ed White looked in. He thought there must be something the matter. There wasn't. Everything, he saw, was fine.

High Desert

I

María Mulrooney did not look at all like the twelve-year-old he had seen at the Gunlock, all wild dark eyes and gangling arms and legs and excited as a new colt. Six years had passed since he had visited the big ranch to buy breed stock for his new spread on the Mojave, and the picture had changed. And a big idea hit him.

Dan Halliday was a man who made his own luck, good or bad. The change in María Mulrooney did not reach him personally. He let his eyelids almost close to cover the look of a gold miner who has turned up a heavy nugget. He stood studying her as he would appraise a fine horse he intended to buy.

She was tall now, as tall as her Spanish mother, with the same olive and smoothly oval face and full dark mouth. She had a woman's ripe breasts and hips—but the big eyes were on a more predatory quest than Olivia's had been. Their expression was only partly veiled by training.

The Mulrooney women were handsome, and the daughter gave Halliday the same quickness of breath that the mother had given him six years before, although he had not dared to cast even an unguarded glance at the older woman. No man took risks with the women of Mike

Mulrooney. Comparing the daughter to the mother now, seeing them so alike, Halliday wondered if old Mike had left anything of himself in his girl. Perhaps what he saw in her eyes was her inheritance from her father—if so, Halliday had really bitten off a job.

Old Mike Mulrooney at sixty had still been a dangerous enemy, although a solid friend. His formidable history had set the pattern. He had killed an arresting officer in Ireland, escaped to the States, and walked West. During the Gold Rush he had fought claim-jumpers and bandits, and, when he had worked out his mine, he had drifted south through the great valley of the San Joaquín, looking for land, pursuing a dream of empire.

He had gotten his start by marrying Olivia and taking over the management of the Rancho Aquina, her family's holding, but keeping the place had not been easy. It had been a bad time. Without Mike's strong will, his courage and ruthless willingness to fight with every tool at hand, the property would have gone the way of so many other Spanish acres.

The native *Californios* were an easy-going lot, harassed by squatters, swindled by land agents, browbeaten by the land commissioners sent from faraway Washington to rule on the validity of their grants from the Spanish king. The commissioners more often than not sided with the Yankee plunderers pouring into the state with the single aim of getting theirs, no matter who was cheated in the process.

Mike Mulrooney had been a match for them all. His riders had run off the squatters at gun point, or killed them if they chose to make a stand. He had driven the crooked land agents out of the country and carried his fight with the land commissioners all the way to Washington to establish his title. He changed the name of the ranch to Gunlock, the name by which the Yankees called the mountain that rose behind the *hacienda,* figuring that the English word would give pause to thieves and swindlers, make them more apt to leave the place alone.

From there he had spread, grabbing land in his own turn from those who had stolen it from his neighbors, until the Gunlock had no rival in all the valley of the Santa Marguerita.

Riding through the rolling miles on that last cattle-buying trip had given Dan Halliday a jealous thrill. And now Olivia was dead and Mike Mulrooney was dead— thrown from a horse they said—and ownership of the whole vast spread rested with this girl before him, standing tense beside the mother superior in the reception hall of the mission.

The mission was very old, one of the first built in central California. The buildings had been abandoned during the years when the Mexican government had driven out the Church in fear of its power over the people. But with the advent of the Americans the *padres* and the nuns had come back.

Halliday's only interest in the place was that it harbored María Mulrooney and gave sanction to this confrontation, and that the *padre* was here, handy. From this moment on, his luck was up to him. The girl—the way she looked—was pure dividend.

His first elation under control, he turned to the mother superior. He surprised her watching María and himself, her clear, smooth face creased with deep doubt. He read her mind as she consigned the problem of Dan Halliday to a higher tribunal. Halliday's meeting with María came under the heading of unusual procedure, and she had nothing in her cloistered experience to guide her yet. Halliday had been to the *padre,* and the *padre* had said he was dependable. The situation was out of her hands.

Halliday encouraged her with his warmest smile, a smile that more worldly women had often succumbed to, empty of guile or calculation. He dipped his head deferentially to the girl.

He said softly: "I am sorry, María, that it took so long to get here. We had to move slowly."

He was running a risk but the nun's uneasiness made risk necessary and he felt that his luck was high. He watched the girl's eyes widen, then narrow with quick thought.

She did not speak. Another mark to her credit. He knew how surprised she must be at the turn of events, yet she did not give away the game by some startled word. As a precaution, though, he looked again at the nun and spoke before either woman could interrupt.

"Thank you for bringing her, Sister. May I ask one favor . . . a few minutes alone to become reacquainted? The *padre* told you we haven't seen each other in some years?"

She showed a marked hesitation as she seemed mentally to cross herself. She looked long at him, at his six-foot-three height, his lean, sun-blackened face, his firm chin, and piercing blue eyes, his too-personal smile. Then, without speaking, she dropped her glance, sighed, and walked out. The heavy plank door that filled the arch in the thick mud wall closed behind her. He waited until the latch clicked. He used the time to glance around and assure himself that no other quiet, black-robed figure stood recessively among the furniture.

The room was large, forty-by-twenty, and ran across the whole front of the building. The stone floor showed through the scattering of dry reeds that carpeted it. The walls held two religious paintings, and the figure of the Virgin stood in a niche at the far end. The furniture was as scant as the decoration, built of split-oak branches, seated with woven cowhide strips, products of the Indian neophytes who had served the early *padres* as half converts, half slaves.

When he was sure that he was alone with the girl, Dan Halliday widened his mouth to a grin and held out a hand. "Come here, María."

She took three smooth steps toward him but stopped beyond his reach. Her eyes met his squarely. They showed him an inner argument—an innate promise and an overlay of suspicion, as if she no longer gave her trust to the world. But her voice, hardly to be heard in its low volume, joined him in conspiracy and her lips barely moved.

"We're watched. They're listening. Why are you here?"

He dropped his own voice, dropped his smile, and put an earnest concern into his face. "You do remember me!"

She fought the grin that parted her full lips for an instant. "The wild Texan. My father called you that once after you rode away."

"A great man, your father."

Her eyes kindled, flashed with a hard light. "He admired you. He said you were as he was at your age . . . a man who took what he wanted and asked no favors." A warning lurked in her tone that nothing he would do could fool her much. "Did you call me out of my prayers to talk about Mike?"

He shook his head. "You like it here?"

The dark eyes darkened. "Does a prisoner like jail?"

"That was the question I pondered some." He smiled again, sharing her secret with her. "And I know a way to get you out. I told the *padre* you were promised to me, that Mike had given us permission to marry when you were eighteen." Watching the face that did not change expression, he added: "You don't seem surprised."

"I've learned to keep my counsel. And there is an eye behind the small hole above that picture. Answer a question . . . I know you didn't come here only to rescue me. What do you expect to gain for yourself? The ranch?"

He all but caught his breath audibly. This was, indeed, Mike Mulrooney's daughter, with a mind like a sharp knife and the courage to aim a strike directly home. He was glad that he could answer with at least a partial truth.

"We've a drought on the Mojave," he said. "Bad drought. I've got two thousand head of cattle starving, dying for lack of water. There's plenty of both feed and water on the Gunlock. I'm offering you a deal, a way to get out of here and take control of what is yours. In return, I want to throw my herd on your ranch and hold it there until my own place gets enough rain."

He saw hope flame in her eyes. Then the flesh of her cheeks drew back, giving emphasis to the high bone structure, and her lips pressed against her white teeth. She came toward him, almost against him, in one violent step—and for a moment he thought her anger was against him, and he cursed himself for blundering. Then her voice came with an acid strength.

"You're asking for a fight with Bruce Alban? Do you know anything about that man?"

"Your uncle? A little."

The way she looked now, as if she could claw the eyes out of a tiger, the furious energy that vibrated from her shook him harder than her quiet beauty had done. His fingers curled, aching to reach for her. He forced himself under control, kept talking to ride out his own inward storm.

"Your father left Gunlock to you, but he made Alban trustee until you were twenty-one or married. I gather Alban wants to keep you here as long as he can. I don't think he intends ever to let you have your ranch. Do you?"

"I do not. Are you man enough to take it from him? Let me tell you about him. He was a gambler. He married my father's sister and weaseled into the ranch because he was clever and good with figures . . . which Mike was not. I did the accounts until Alban came, so I know." She paused. "I was fifteen when Mike died, and right after that Alban came to my room . . . to comfort me, he said. He put his hands on me. He threw me on the bed. I fought him, but he was too big. He kept gasping that he'd get rid of my aunt, that he was going to marry me. He said I drove him wild. He said I was headed for trouble, the way I acted with the crew . . . that I was old enough for love and that I shouldn't waste it on hired hands."

Halliday knew fleeting sympathy for the uncle. He could picture María at fifteen and it was no chore to guess that she had been as provocative as she was this instant, a heady and tantalizing creature surrounded by a society of young, hot-blooded riders.

Then she was rushing on, her sweet breath—hot with anger—brushing his face with the violence escaping her. "I hated him. I had to get away. There was a boy . . . a rider, a friend. I told him. The next night he had horses ready and I sneaked out of the bedroom. We headed for the hills . . . toward Santa Barbara, where I had relatives. Alban chased us and caught us. He hung Tom up by his thumbs and used a bullwhip on him, nearly cut him to ribbons. Then he brought me here and told the nuns I was too promiscuous to trust outside. They listened to him and shut me up. I don't blame them . . . they love me, I know that. But they don't understand."

She flung up her head, stretching her fine throat. Her dark eyes were wide and reminded Halliday of a proud young mare, wild and free on a wind-blown hill.

She repeated: "They don't understand. Mike Mulrooney taught me to love life, to take it and live it all, and never to fear it. Bruce Alban has twisted what my father taught to shame me and coop me up here to steal my ranch. That's the man you're choosing to fight. Do you still want to try?"

He let his grin spread steadily. No softness remained in it. "More than ever . . . now that I've seen you."

Her suspicion came back. It made her frown. "How did you know I was here? What gave you the idea of coming?"

"Tom stopped at my place last month. He's still pretty crippled. He told me the story. It seemed my only chance to save my herd."

She looked up at him for a long moment, an eternity to him. Then he saw her make her decision.

"All right. I'll marry you. Get me my ranch back, Dan Halliday. Drive Bruce Alban out of the country or kill him."

He reached slowly for her hands and she gave them to him. And not until he held them tightly did he suggest that he wanted something more.

"It's only fair to tell you that I haven't much of a crew with me. Just my partner and four riders . . . and they aren't fighting men."

The words did not faze her. Her smile came as cold and hard as his. "There are fighters on the Gunlock . . . *vaqueros* whose people worked for my mother's family for a hundred years. Men trained by Mike Mulrooney . . . men who loved him. Get me home, Dan Halliday. You'll have all the help you need."

11

The *padre* did not actually believe that marriages were made in heaven, although he wanted to. He was a gentle man who to the best of his ability lived in a cloister of his own making, ignoring the bitterness, the greed, the excesses of the wild frontier that surrounded him. He would not have chosen Dan Halliday as the husband for María. He sensed a latent and disturbing violence in this dark-faced man. But he was realistic enough to know that, as heiress to one of the country's greatest ranches, she was a tempting prize. He also knew that she needed a strong man to hold her.

Finally he did not trust her uncle. The story Bruce Alban had told him when he brought the girl to the mission had distressed the *padre* by the character of its charge. He had later learned that María Mulrooney, indeed, had a wild streak—but he had never been able to believe she was the wanton Alban claimed her to be.

He joined María Mulrooney and Dan Halliday as man and wife with hopeful relief and, in his own mind, shifted the responsibility for the girl's well-being onto the powerful shoulders of the new husband. He did not at all guess, as they kneeled before him, that to Mike Mulrooney's daughter this was no more than a marriage of convenience.

Or that she resented her need to go through this ceremony in order to free herself.

Her strongest emotion at the moment was one that had sustained her through all her time of confinement—a burning hatred of her uncle. It sprang less from the physical violence to which he had subjected her than from his seizure of the ranch that was her birthright. She meant to bring him low, to whip him—to see him killed if possible. She appraised the man beside her with no other heat. He was big enough for her purpose—six feet four, she guessed. The shockingly blue eyes in the sun-darkened face suggested to her that enough harsh strength of purpose lived in him to make him an adequate tool—and a tool was all she considered him.

She resented Dan Halliday almost as much as she resented her uncle—but Halliday she resented because she needed him. She did not like to admit need. Halliday had diagnosed her trouble—and the anger that drove her and sought to turn it to his own advantage. This was easy for her to understand. But as she murmured the words after the *padre,* she thought fiercely that she and Halliday must have a showdown. As soon as she was safely clear of the mission, Halliday must be made to understand that his rights on the Gunlock were limited to graze for his herd, and only until such time as he could return his animals to his own range. Gunlock was hers. She had not the slightest intention of sharing it with anyone. Once she had rallied her father's riders and rid the place—perhaps the world—of Bruce Alban, she would no longer need this man who had just been declared her husband.

She permitted Halliday's kiss. She smiled and in a seemly gesture sought comfort in the arms of the sisters who took her away to change to traveling costume. She turned at the chapel door and glanced back with a sense of unreality. A man who she had met only once before was now united with her in marriage.

She expected to meet his smile, to give him one in return, no matter how false its interpretation might be—but he was not looking at her. His whole attention was on the priest. For some reason she could not define, the fact hurt her. She felt a rising anger against the callousness of this big, self-assured man.

She wore the plain, dark dress that had been her uniform at the mission, high at the neck, long sleeved, a concealing, unprovocative dress. Now, to the consternation of the nuns, she chose a full, bright skirt, wide enough to permit her to ride a man's saddle astride. She chose a light blouse with no sleeves at all, a thing that barely hung on her shoulders and was scooped deeply enough in front for the soft crease between her pale, swelling breasts to show above the fabric. The dress was a challenge. She knew that Halliday could not ignore it, and took a perverse pleasure in the knowledge. Not that she wanted him—but she did not intend to let him put his attention elsewhere.

But when they mounted their horses later and rode after the herd that had passed the mission gardens early in the morning, Halliday barely glanced at her. He immediately turned his eyes to the sweeping horizon and rode, scrutinizing the empty land as if in quest of imminent danger.

She hid her annoyance and they rode in silence. She had spent more of her childhood on horseback than she had in walking and sat her animal with an easy confidence that matched any man's.

The steady loping gait of the animals ate at the miles to the looming heights of the Tehachapi. She smelled the herd even before she saw the cloud of its passage. The dust lingered in the hot, windless air—she and Halliday rode through it to overtake the slowly moving train as it headed into the long cañon draw that wound to the pass above.

Halliday spoke to the man riding drag, smothered in the roiling yellow dust stirred up by the hoofs of the dolorous cattle. Cap Norton was a slight man. His body looked withered and underfed beneath the stained, worn shirt and faded pants. His eyes were so light as to seem white against leather-dark skin, and his mouth was a wicked slash, without humor to ease its cynical smirk.

He raised a hand in a laconic salute as Halliday and María pulled up beside him. He lowered the red neckerchief that had been protecting his nostrils from the flying grit. His pale eyes, holding no more feeling than a reptile's, raked across María, seeming to strip the bright clothing from her.

She flushed under the penetration of his gaze and barely nodded as Halliday made the introduction.

"So, you're married." A graveling, mocking note echoed in Norton's voice.

"We're married."

Dan Halliday's tone was short. He had never had any personal fondness for his partner. Cap Norton was not a likable man. He had, in fact, boasted that he had not a single real friend in the world. But he was a good cattleman, a man without fear, and he had had enough money to help stock Halliday's Mojave ranch. Halliday had met him in Mexico and the partnership had been forged over a lonely campfire deep in the Sierra Madre del Norte, when Halliday had told Norton of the desert ranch he had inherited from a cousin.

Halliday did not miss Norton's appraisal of María. He swung away and led her down the flank of the faltering herd. Her voice startled his thoughts as she broke her long silence.

"Do you really think you can get these animals across the Tehachapi?"

"We'll get them over." His voice was tight with his determination. "Do you understand now why I need a place to run them?"

She had never seen such scrawny stock in the lush valleys of the Gunlock. Her antagonism against this man, who continued to ignore her, gave way before a recognition of the plight of the animals, gaunted to nothing more than walking skeletons. That they could move at all amazed her. But they were pushing forward up the cañon without need of urging from the riders. The leaders had scented the water at the crest and would have broken into a run had they had the strength.

The newlyweds rode past the other members of the crew. Halliday was conscious of the curious eyes that followed him. The men were in little better shape than the animals, a nondescript crew without pride and, he knew, without loyalty. They stayed with Halliday only because in the burned-out country they had left there were no other jobs and because the creaking chuck wagon still carried food—flour, beans, and jerked meat. They had not been paid in weeks and would go over the hill without notice, given any chance to better themselves.

"A sorry outfit," María said with a touch of impatience. "You didn't give me much of a trade, Dan Halliday."

He looked at her squarely for the first time since they had left the mission and his grin suddenly changed his face. "We make a fine pair, don't we? I told you I didn't have a fighting crew."

She fell silent again, thinking. For her purpose it was as

well that he did not have fighting men. He would have to depend fully on her father's Mexican riders to turn the task of taking Gunlock away from Bruce Alban.

"I don't like your partner," she told him. "I don't like the way he looks at me."

Halliday shrugged. "Cap doesn't have much use for women."

"Can you trust him?"

Halliday thought about this for a long moment, then lifted his shoulders again. "As long as I haven't got anything he can steal."

He pushed his horse to a faster pace. They passed the eager leaders struggling up the grade, passed the point man, and pressed on until they crossed the summit. María stayed at his side, a growing unease gripping her, a feeling that, although she had escaped from the mission, she was still far from safe.

It was nearly dark when the first of the cattle reached the brush-screened stream on the far side of the divide, on the slope that let down into the valley of the Kern. The bawling of the stock filled the evening air as the thirsty steers massed and shoved at each other to reach the trickle in the boulder-strewn bed.

The riders made no effort to hold them back—there was not enough moisture for the animals to founder. And although the narrow valley held little feed, beasts could be counted on not to stray from the thread of the first water they had known in three days.

The battered chuck wagon had been pulled onto a small rocky point above the surging cattle. The evening fire made a bright spot of light in the growing darkness. The cook was busy with his pan biscuits and the riders lounged back from the blaze, nursing cups of black coffee, watching María from eyes that held a stark, animal hunger.

She sat alone on a rock some twenty feet from the wagon, gazing out across the darkening hills, remembering nights such as this when she had camped with her father. An awareness crept into her that someone was near, some attention concentrated on her. She turned. Cap Norton stood fifteen feet away.

When he knew that he had been seen, he came forward with a quiet, cat-like step and squatted at her side. He asked in his grating voice: "You real pleased to be married?"

She would have liked to ignore him, but she wanted no trouble until she was safely on the Gunlock with the loyal *vaqueros* around her. She said noncommittally: "It's a little strange."

"So?" Norton had pulled a knife from its sheath and balanced on the balls of his feet, flipping the knife idly, watching the glinting point bite into the ground, over and over. He did not look at her. His whole attention was given to his game with the knife.

"Kind of jumped at the chance to grab a man, didn't you, baby?"

Hot anger flashed through her, and with an effort she checked its expression, knowing instinctively that he was deliberately trying to goad her—although she did not quite understand the reason behind his words.

She said levelly: "Did you expect me not to marry Dan?"

He shook his head. "Never expect a woman to do anything . . . at least, anything I'd admire."

"You must have had very bad experiences with women."

Norton's chuckle carried a rattlesnake's warning. "I have. And they've had some with me. I've been watching you, missy, for the last hour . . . studying you, you might say . . . and I can almost see your mind working. Here you got a couple of starving cowmen who can pull your ranch out of the fire for you. Right?"

She said slowly: "My agreement was with Dan. I had none with you."

"You do now, although you don't know it, maybe. Danny and I are partners. What happens to him happens to me. Only difference is, Dan is easy-going. Me, I like all the things written down, each and every one. So, let's me and you start now. Right?"

She did not answer. She kept her eyes on the knife blade as it made its arc in the air and landed accurately, the point burying and reburying itself in the flinty soil.

Norton's lean hand moved with rhythmic grace, retrieving the knife, flipping it again and again. Something deadly was suggested by the monotonous repetition. Presently she thought it might be the blade was an extension of the man's hand. María watched with hypnotic fascination, hearing Norton's words, yet trying to reject them.

"Let's look at it this way," he was saying. "You don't rate control of the Gunlock until you're married. Right?"

She did not speak.

"So, now you're married. And according to the rules all you got to do is ride in and take over. That is, if your uncle lets you."

"Dan will see that he does."

"Sure, Dan will see to it . . . because there ain't a man in the country much better with a gun than Danny Halliday. So, Dan puts you on your ranch. You round up all your daddy's old *vaqueros* and you run your ever-loving uncle out of the territory. Then what?"

She said in a small voice: "What do you mean?"

"Just what I said. What happens to Dan then? What happens to me? What happens to our stock?"

"You'll be taken care of. The agreement is that I will furnish pasture until you can go back to your own land." She pulled her eyes away from the knife, rose quickly, caught up her saddle blanket, and moved away, climbing a little draw until she found a small depression screened by brush.

Norton remained where he was, watching her go. His pale eyes glinted in the coming darkness. His mouth was a dissatisfied, petulant line. He did not move until Halliday came from the creek, where he had been pulling some of the weaker animals out of the water.

Halliday brought a cup of coffee from the chuck wagon and sank down beside his partner. "We've had the worst of it. Tomorrow there'll be water all the way down. And then we pick up the Kern."

Norton made no sign that he heard. He continued to flip the narrow blade as if his life depended on keeping the rhythm. Halliday watched for a moment, letting his annoyance show. "Put that damn' toad stabber away."

Norton did not even pause in his game.

Halliday was suddenly aware that his wife, who he had seen here a little while ago, was not now in sight. "Where's María?"

Norton gestured with the knife point toward the draw. "Took her gear and hiked up there."

"Without supper?"

"Maybe she wasn't hungry." Norton pitched the knife once more, drew the blade between his thumb and finger to clean it of the dust. He shoved it into the sheath at his belt.

Halliday watched him narrowly. "What did you say to her?"

Norton's eyes glinted wickedly. "I asked her if she was pleased to be married in such a hurry."

71

"Damn it." Halliday threw the dregs of his coffee into the brush. "I want you to leave her alone. She's just a kid fresh out of a convent. She's been through a hell of a lot and she's scared enough."

Norton grinned sardonically. "She's a kid, you can say. But when they look like that, they're ripe. And she ain't helpless or she's as helpless as a mountain cat. She's sitting up there right now trying to figure out just how she will get rid of us as soon as she's sure she's in control of Gunlock."

"I don't believe you."

"You don't believe me. You're a big man, know all about handling a woman, think because a *padre* said some hocus-pocus over the two of you she's your slave. You don't know from rule one about women."

Halliday sounded exasperated: "Cap, from the first time I suggested we take over Gunlock, you've been obstinate as a mule."

"Oh, so, you are taking over Gunlock? Does your wife know that? From what she said, I got the idea she thought the deal was temporary. You were going to run her uncle off, and, in return, we could pasture our steers until we could move back to the Mojave."

Dan Halliday shrugged. "I let her think so. I was in too much of a hurry to go into the whole thing."

"Then you'd better let her think different," Norton growled, "before you and me wind up at one end of a rope with her happy *vaqueros* pulling on the other end."

III

"I brought you something to eat."

She had heard him coming up the draw, boots scuffing over the rocky ground. She had sat up tensely, wrapped the blanket around her bare shoulders. She held it together tightly.

The night was warm. The air still held the heat of the day as it rose from the valley below. The only sound other than the footsteps was the restless moving of the cattle along the creek, hugging the damp, brushy banks as if afraid that, if they ventured farther than a few feet from the water, the precious moisture would vanish.

She tried to stop Halliday's approach. She called out: "I'm not hungry!"

He paid no attention. He came on, rounding the screen of brush, his dark shadow coming into sight just before he dropped to his knees at her side. He juggled a plate piled with beans, pan biscuits, stewed jerked meat in one hand, a cup of coffee in the other. "We've got a hard day tomorrow. Eat."

She was ready to refuse. Then she guessed that accepting the food was the quickest way to be rid of him. She reached for the plate, and lifted a forkful to her mouth. One side of the blanket slipped down her shoulder. Halliday had a fleeting glimpse of one pale breast before she snatched the cover up again. She hunched over, continuing to eat, the blanket held in place by the tension of her posture and the weight of the plate in her lap. Silence grew between them and she sensed something new in it, a sudden strain that had not been there before.

To break it, she said: "Your partner tried to frighten me. He came over and watched me as a lizard watches a fly. He was playing with that knife as if it were a lizard's tongue . . . threatening me."

"Don't mind Cap." Halliday spoke softly. "He's naturally suspicious. He thinks you mean to use us to get your ranch, and then throw us out."

She set the plate aside awkwardly. "I intend to keep our bargain."

"I expected that. I hoped for something more."

Her head came up sharply. "The marriage is in name only. That was understood."

"I know. But think about it. You can't hold onto Gunlock alone, even with the *vaqueros*. There will be men after it, worse men than your uncle. You need me, María. And I. . . ." His hand snaked out, closing over her shoulder. He deliberately brushed down the edge of the blanket so that his fingers closed on her warm skin. She saw him react as if he had touched a bolt of lightning. His grip glued to her, fused by a current stronger than any she had ever experienced. His breath sucked in and with a convulsive gesture he pulled her toward him.

She was quick. Before he realized it, she was out of his grasp, breaking free, rolling to her hands and knees, her eyes enormous on him. The blanket had fallen away and she was a naked statue, her young body glowing in the moonlight, her long dark hair falling like black water on both sides of her face, veiling her breasts. "Leave me alone."

He laughed at her. The hot taste of musk in his mouth matched the musky scent that reached him from her exposed body, a perfume to enclose them, separate the two of them from the rest of the night. He reached for her again.

She leaped to her feet. Her eyes fled to the limp pile of her clothes on the rock nearby. She ran toward them. He caught her arms from behind and lifted her clear of the ground. He turned her struggling body in mid-air and crushed it to him.

She did not cry out. Instead she immediately ceased to fight. She hung quietly in his arms. He felt the warm yield of her breasts against his chest, the warm length of her down his legs.

He bent his head. His mouth searched for hers. She tried to twist her face, to escape the kiss. He was too strong. He held her in one encircling arm, using his free hand to force her chin up. His mouth covered hers.

She bit his lip. Her teeth met his flesh solidly.

He instinctively jerked away, cursing her, his hold on her relaxing. She used the moment to wrench free once more and catch her balance. Next she had turned and was racing up the draw, in spite of her panic a thing of grace and beauty flowing through the moonlight.

He was after her like a panther. He was gripped now by a compounded passion—sexual urge heightened by anger— but beyond both drummed the knowledge that he had to conquer, had to dominate her or lose his whole gamble. He had not needed Norton to tell him so.

Her bare feet were cut by the sharp flinty surface of the baked earth, and he caught her easily in a few lunging leaps.

She had struck a steep embankment and was trying to scramble up its side. His hand clutched an ankle. He yanked her back down the slope. The rocks made long, reddening grooves down her legs.

She fell on top of him, fighting wildly, clawing at his eyes with long, strong fingers, yet her only sounds were a gasping strangle in her throat.

And then he had gripped her with painful tightness in the crook of one arm while his other hand pulled open his shirt, peeled away his clothes. He said: "Bitch."

Her nails dug a long furrow down his cheek.

He hit her with the flat of his palm. "Stop it before I break your neck."

She uttered a moan, a gurgling exhalation. Her twisting struggles ceased and she made no further protest. He spun back to the blanket, held her down with his weight.

Dan Halliday had been raised on the Texas border and the women he had known had been those who hung around the log saloons, danced in the *cantinas* below the line. There was no gentleness in him and he was not gentle now. He took her as he had taken everything else in life, with a full-bodied violence, whetted by long months of enforced denial.

At first she gave no response. This much, at least, was true of the legend surrounding her—he was not her first man, even discounting what she had told him of her uncle. She lay limp as a sack of grain, as if she were not conscious of what was happening to her. At last her body stirred in spite of herself, the command of nature overwhelmed the dictates of her mind. Suddenly she was meeting him, striving toward a realization even as he was striving, groaning now in her effort, then crying out as her fulfillment came and the nails of her fingers bit into the skin of his shoulders. He clapped his hand across her mouth, cutting off the sound, and collapsed against her. They lay inert, surfeited, their flesh welded together by their heat, clinging to each other as if nothing on earth could ever part them again.

She was gripped by a feeling of complete unreality, as if she were another person, looking on, observing the emotional tempest of two people who did not relate to her in any way.

She had hated her uncle and had begun by hating this man who now held her tightly in his powerful arms. And she still hated him. But somewhere in the past few moments, she had gained a knowledge of life that had not been hers before. She had intended to use Dan Halliday for her own purposes and then discard him when those purposes had been served. But she had feared him, too, and had been unsure of how far she could control him. She no longer entertained that fear. In his raw passion, in his desperate need she had found a secret—in sex lay her strength, in the giving or withholding of her favors.

That she had herself been aroused she realized and coolly judged with some calculating part of her mind. She was physically too weak to battle men, but from this moment on she knew that she could use her charms in battle—to sway at least this man to her command. She had a weapon worthy of her aims—and wielding it could give her the same pleasure a man took in more violent arms.

Halliday experienced a sudden rush of tenderness for this girl that he had never known for any other woman. He moved, sliding one arm beneath her head, bent and kissed her gently, aware for the first time of the stinging burn in his lips where her teeth had cut through. The anger that had seized him at that moment was gone. He kissed her again, finding an open acceptance, a warm sweetness. He lowered his face to her breasts, kissing first one, then the other. He felt her stir with response. He knew freedom and yet a bondage—both were totally new in his experience. He raised his lips again to hers.

He whispered: "I love you, María."

She did not reply, and he knew a curious sense of loss. He felt denied, rebuffed. And then her hands were on his shoulders, tugging at him, pulling his weight to her. She guided him back to their love. Not to the wild, furious frenzy of their first meeting. Their second seeking for consummation held something that had been lacking in their earlier violence—it became a confirmation of what each of them had discovered about the other earlier. Eternity telescoped into an instant. They rested. And the storm broke anew. Much later they slept.

Halliday awoke first. He slipped his arm from under his wife without arousing her, found his clothes, and dressed quietly. He brought her skirt and blouse, dropped them beside her, and stood looking down at her beauty. At last he draped the blanket gently over her.

He moved down toward the stream. He passed the wagon, found that the cook had the breakfast fire blazing. His crew was already working the cattle from the brakes, making ready to head them down the grade toward the distant valley of the Kern. Half a dozen of the weaker animals had died during the night, but to Halliday's practiced eye the rest seemed in better shape than they had been at the start of the drive.

He found a place up the creek where the stock had not muddied the water. He stripped, waded into the shallow stream, and lay down, washing the blood and dirt from his face and body. His lip was swollen to double its natural size, and he soaked if for some time, feeling the chill water eat at the throb.

When he came out to dress, he found Norton on the bank, silently watching him. The pale eyes noted the lip and the scratches on the dark face. Norton grinned wickedly.

"Heavy night, huh?"

Halliday said shortly: "There has to be some misunderstanding before two people can live together."

Norton frowned, changed the subject. "How long do you figure until we get down to the valley where there's some grass?"

"Three, four days."

Norton looked away at the line of scrawny animals heading down the narrow pass. "We're just about going to make it. If we have trouble when we get to the Gunlock, we'll lose the bunch."

"We'll have no trouble." Halliday was filled with a new confidence. He went back to the wagon, filled two plates, and took them up the draw to where his wife still slept. He stood over her, smiling and thinking: *Everything is working into my hands. If I'm lucky . . . she's pregnant . . . there will be no more question about my taking over the ranch.* This was heady thought, one to make a man feel twice as big as he really was.

He laughed aloud, waking her, saying: "Did they let you sleep all day at the mission? You'll have to learn that a ranch doesn't work that way."

She opened her eyes. She had been dreaming of the days when her father had been alive and vital, when no cares or problems had beset the women of Mike Mulrooney. Suddenly she was awake, staring up at the man she had married. For an instant the memory of the night brought quick

79

anger. Then she veiled her thoughts and arranged a smile.

"You should have gotten me up earlier."

He handed her the plate, squatted by her side, and they ate. Then she rose, pulled on her skirt, dropped the blouse over her head, and began to comb her hair with her fingers.

He admired her openly. "You brought me luck," he said. "We lost less than half a dozen steers, and in three days we should be down on good grass. I'm riding ahead, to Bakersfield, to see if I can pick up some fresh horses. The ones we've been using are about through."

Quick fear jumped into her eyes. "Take me with you."

He shook his head. "Bakersfield is no place for a woman. All the scum of the valley headquarters there. You'll be all right with the boys and Cap. There's not one of them dares to lay a hand on something that belongs to me."

Her temper flared. For a long time, it had lurked close to the surface. She crowded it down, and said meekly— "Whatever you think best."—and followed him down to where the cook was already loading his wagon to pull out.

IV

Bakersfield squatted on the flat California plain, a dozen miles from where the Kern boiled out of its cañon to lose most of its water in the shifting valley sand. It was an unlovely place of sun-bleached board buildings, of adobes gradually melting into the soil of which they were made. The population varied with every passing sun. It was made up partly of native Spanish-speaking people of mixed Indian blood, partly of toughs who had been run out of the railroad towns to the north.

This was the end of rail. The line had come down the wide sweep of the San Joaquín, but the engineers had not yet solved the crossing of the rocky barrier, the Tehachapi, that separated this flat land from the settlements around Los Angeles and San Diego.

The outlaws controlled the town and the countryside around it. The scattered ranchers were too few to stand against them and the Spanish people kept to themselves, staying within the crooked streets of Old Town while the brush jumpers, thieves, murderers hurrahed the main street and drove off every lawman sent against them.

Leaving the herd to descend the pass, Halliday rode into

the sorry hole at evening, put up his mount at Harker's livery.

He asked the hostler: "Where can I buy half a dozen ponies?"

The man shrugged. He was slight, sunburned, well on in years. Any liking for life seemed long gone out of him.

"Don't know."

Halliday looked out through the wide open door of the barn runway and into the pole corral behind the building. Some thirty horses slowly circled the enclosure.

"Those for sale?"

"You'll have to ask Gabe Pierson."

Halliday knew the name. Pierson was a widely known outlaw, wanted in most of the states of the West. That he now lived openly in Bakersfield under his own name was an indication of the lawless character of the town. If the animals were Gabe Pierson's, they were no doubt stolen.

Halliday could not afford to be choosy. The mounts his hands were riding were, if anything, worse than the cattle they drove. And a man on foot was no match for a range steer.

"Where'll I find Pierson?"

The old man shrugged. "If he's in town . . . I'd say at the Fremont. If he ain't . . . your guess is as good as mine."

Halliday turned up the wooden sidewalk that had been built a foot above the powdery dust of the rutted street. The Fremont stood on the town's main corner, across from the single-storied bank, the only bank to be found in that portion of the state. A train hooted from the yellow station and, with a scuffing noise, moved out its mixed cargo of freight cars and a passenger coach. Halliday paused to watch it move past the loading pens and head out on the straight line of track toward Stockton and Sacramento, 350 miles north. He turned and strode toward the saloon.

Horses stood at most of the hitch rails. Wagons and buckboards were pulled up before the three general stores. People filled the street, mostly male. He saw only two women—farm women perched on high wagon seats while their men carried out supplies. Faded females, their faces shaded from the blaze of the desert sun, their eyes peering from under a cloth bonnet. Their dresses were as weathered as their skins. It was not a woman's town. The ranch wives stayed carefully away from the vicinity of the four saloons, the most prosperous establishments of the town.

The Fremont was by far the most pretentious of the four—a one-story structure thirty feet along the street, forty feet deep. Behind it a row of one-room shanties housed girls employed in the bar.

Their job was to sit with the customers, dance with them to the tinny piano, and prevail on them to buy as many drinks as they could hold. What they did in their off hours was up to them. As long as they did their stints in the saloon and paid their rents on the cribs out back, Kate Wormack asked no questions and permitted no one else to ask.

Halliday had met Kate once—when he had come through on his cattle-buying trip—but he did not expect her to remember him and was surprised when she did.

A clutch of men stood at the bar and two of the poker tables were going when he came in. It was near the supper hour, but the summer sun still hung like a red-hot glassy ball on the horizon and its dusky glow seeped into the saloon. No one paid any attention to Halliday except Kate Wormack. She stood at the end of the counter, talking to the bartender. Kate missed little of what happened in the big room. She was big but curvaceous, with generous hips. Her swelling breasts were accented by a low-cut dress. She was dark-haired and her black eyes snapped. A trace of Indian was in the set of her cheek bones. Her mouth was a crimson slash. She was a sumptuously attractive woman, although not as young as she once had been.

She pushed away from the bar, walked between the row of men hanging on the counter and the poker tables behind them, her hips swaying but her posture as erect as if she carried a basket on her head. She paused before Halliday as he stood inside the swinging doors to have his look at the room.

"Hello, Texas."

He smiled down at her, strangely pleased. "You've a good memory, Kate. I was through here only once."

"I know. Missed you. I seldom forget a man set up as you are."

His grin widened. "Quit it. You're only trying to sell rotgut."

She made a contemptuous gesture with a hand adorned by three flashing diamond rings. The glittering arc took in girls seated with customers at the tables, tucked in at the bar between others. "I keep them to do that. You'll have better. Come on and sit down." She swung away, leading him to an empty table, signaling the bartender as she passed him. He reached the table almost as soon as Kate did. He brought a bottle and two glasses, poured drinks, and went back to his post, saying nothing.

Kate lifted her glass but did not carry it to her lips. She toyed with it, looking across its rim at Halliday. "What brings you out to this stink hole?"

He toasted her with a lift of his drink. "Horses."

"What about horses?"

He told her about the Mojave drought, about the herd Norton was bringing across the mountains, his worry that the crew would presently be on foot.

Kate leaned back in her chair, hooking a firm, bare arm over the back. "You've got nerve, driving a herd through here. There're twenty men in this room, fifty or sixty more out in the hills, and all of them would love nothing better than to lift your cattle the first dark night."

He grinned wryly. "They aren't worth stealing, unless you want the hides. No self-respecting rustler would give them a second glance. Do you know where I can find Gabe Pierson?"

She arched a questioning eyebrow. "What do you want with him?"

"As I said, horses. There's a bunch at the livery that the hostler said belonged to Pierson."

"He claims them, if that's what you mean by belonging. No, I don't know where Gabe is . . . I haven't seen him in four, five days. He might be anywhere. But I'll ask." She raised her voice so that it carried above the hubbub of the room. "Scotty."

A lean man with a wicked mouth and broken nose detached himself from a girl at the bar and came unhurriedly toward the table. "What is it?"

"Where's Gabe?"

The man's insolent eyes went over Halliday slowly. It was obvious that he did not like strangers. "Who wants to know?"

Kate Wormack did not enjoy being questioned in this tone.

"Texas here wants to buy some horses."

"Know him?"

"If I didn't I wouldn't be asking you."

The thin man kicked out a chair and sank into it. "How many head?"

"Six, eight. If the price is right."

"What would you call a right price?"

"Fifteen dollars."

The man laughed. "We're selling them, not giving them away."

"Who to?"

"Who to what?"

"Who you going to sell them to in this country?"

Scotty rubbed his nose reflectively.

"I'll make it twenty," Halliday said. "That's a lot more than you paid for them."

Anger stirred in Scotty's eyes. "Well, now."

"I don't care where you got them." Halliday's tone was easy. He had no desire to pick a fight with this man. "I'm not wearing a badge. I'll give you one hundred and sixty dollars for eight head. I pick them."

The offer was dangerous in that it represented nearly all the cash he and Norton had left. But horses were imperative. Halliday sat breathless as Scotty thought it over.

Then: "I'll ask Gabe."

"When will that be?"

"When I see him."

With that, Halliday had to be content. Scotty rose and went back to the bar. He made no move toward leaving the room, and Halliday was forced to believe that Gabe Pierson was not in town.

He said: "Not very friendly."

"Scotty?" Kate Wormack laughed, a sound of rich enjoyment. "Scotty fancies himself a badman. He gets away with a lot because of Gabe. For some reason Gabe always backs him up . . . damned if I know why." She tasted her drink.

"Where are you staying?"

Halliday had not even thought of the hotel. He had no money to waste on such luxuries as a bed.

"I'll sleep down at the livery."

"You can't eat down there."

His smile twisted. "I never did make out well on oats. Where would you suggest?"

"Have dinner with me. I get tired of listening to these saddle tramps. It's a relief to see someone who at least looks like a man."

"Thanks."

She ignored his sarcasm. "Funny you never met Gabe down around the border. He headquartered there for four or five years."

"Never did that I remember."

She stood up with an undulating grace. He fumbled in his pocket for money to pay for the drinks, but she shook her head.

"Forget it, Texas. They're on the house." She motioned to the bartender to pick up the bottle and glasses, then led Halliday through the street door and turned along the sidewalk to the side street.

Her house was built of adobe in the Spanish style, with a wall along the street, high and windowless. She pushed open a thick plank door and ushered him into the patio. More flowers bloomed in the curving borders of the stone-paved paths than he had seen in all of California. A small fountain played in the center of a mounded garden. The central figure was a naked girl spewing water from her bronze mouth. He stared at it in amazement, and Kate Wormack laughed.

"You like her?"

He said: "I never saw anything like it."

"Drunken sculptor came down here from Stockton and ran up a bill at the bar," she said. "He did this for me to pay for his liquor. I posed for him."

His eyes widened as he tried to associate the nymph in the little pool with the buxom woman at his side. He tried to sound convincing. "I see the resemblance."

She chortled in appreciation. "The hell you do. You're a poor liar, Texas." She raised her voice in a shout. "Sam, hey, Sam!"

An ancient Chinese servant, who wore his queue coiled neatly around his small head, appeared in one of the doorways that opened on the square patio.

"What you want?"

"Supper. We've got company. Hurry it up, Sam. Bring us a bottle of that mission wine. We'll eat out here." She indicated a table under a pepper tree that spread its branches over one corner of the yard.

Halliday was still looking about him, drinking in the feeling that this was an oasis in the waterless, treeless land around the town.

"Rest yourself," she said, "while I get out of this damned corset."

She left him and climbed an outside stairway to an iron-railed balcony that ran around three sides of the patio. Halliday watched her climb, admiring the firm turn of her legs. Then he went into the kitchen and asked the Chinaman where he could wash. He was shown the bench beyond the rear door. He dipped water from the barrel into a chipped basin. The sun had played on the barrel all day, and he washed in warm water for the first time since leaving his Mojave ranch.

V

When he returned to the patio, Kate was already at the table, pouring amber wine into stemmed glasses. She had exchanged her working costume for a loose wrapper without shape, a tent-like Mother Hubbard. It made her look younger, more feminine, and provocative. She handed him a glass.

"It has to have been a man who invented the corset, and he ought to have one tightened around his head."

"I don't know. Never wore one. Don't intend to." He grinned, watched her raise the wine to her lips and taste it. He followed her example.

The wine had a nutty taste like a good Spanish sherry. Kate ran the pink tip of her tongue around her lips greedily, as if not wanting to miss a single drop.

"Good?"

He bowed his head.

They ate roast chicken cooked with a sauce Halliday could not identify. It had the flavor of almonds. The chicken was served with rice, fluffy, each grain separate from the others, and was followed by small round sugar cakes, an almond in the center of each. They drank tea. He had never tasted it before.

"Sam's a good cook," Kate said. "I stole him from

the Palace in San Francisco."

He looked at her curiously. He asked: "What the hell are you doing in Bakersfield?"

She grimaced, then raised her brows in acceptance of a situation. "My husband was a gambler . . . he started the Fremont. But he was quicker at pulling a card from his sleeve than at pulling a gun. When he got shot, I had to take over this place. It isn't too bad . . . but I get lonesome to be with a decent man once in a while."

The sun was gone now. The patio was blessed with cool shadow.

He hated the idea of leaving it, but said perversely: "Don't you have to go back to the saloon?"

"Joe can run it. Joe's the bartender."

She pulled a sack of tobacco from a pocket of her dress and rolled a cigarette, then offered him the sack and papers. The smoke tasted good after the meal, a meal such as he had seldom eaten in his life. He sat back and relaxed. It was pleasant here behind the thick mud wall, remote as if you were in another country. He had seen houses like this in New Orleans when he had driven a herd of wild Gulf cattle through the swamps to Crescent City.

His cigarette finished, he said reluctantly: "Well, I guess I'd better be going."

Her lip twisted. "Where to? The livery?"

He shrugged. "I've a hunch it's about as good as the hotel."

"Better."

"I'd better go see."

"Why not stay here?"

He looked at her, startled, found her smiling and read the invitation in her dark eyes. She saw his confusion and her smile broadened.

"Don't get me wrong, Texas. I don't work out of the bar the way some of my girls do. I never played the game that way. I'm choosey. But the bed's big and it's clean . . . and better than a pile of hay on the stable floor."

His breath filled his chest as he rose and pulled her to her feet. Her rings were hard against his fingers as his hand closed over hers. He had guessed that she wore nothing under the roomy dress, and knew that he was right the moment his arms went around her. The flesh was firm but yielding to his touch. She lifted her mouth for his kiss, and her lips were a warm circle, putting heat through him.

Some women understand the projection of sex. Kate was one of these. Sex, not love, was the depth of her experience, but it was a considerable depth. His reaction to Kate was entirely different from his feeling toward María. María had wanted either more or less than physical love from him; he was not yet sure of exactly what she wanted, and her surrender to her natural urges had obscured the picture for him. But he had been profoundly moved by her. Kate, he knew, was simply starved for the attention she knew and liked and had been denied too long.

She led him up the ornate stairway and along the balcony to a big corner room. The interior was overpoweringly feminine. The curtains were lace. The bed was covered with a Chinese silk throw of shining gold. Light fell softly from a prismed crystal lamp hanging from the beamed ceiling. She made no gesture toward dimming it. She folded back the gold cloth, then sheets of real linen, turned to face him, and flung the shapeless dress over her head and away.

Where María was strong with youth and promise, Kate was ripe with promises fulfilled. Her hips were large and powerful. Her breasts were big but had not yet begun to sag.

She threw up her head, smiling at him, then asked with impatience: "Are you going to stand there gawking all night?"

He hesitated for the barest moment before he pulled off his shirt and unfastened his belt. She watched him with a connoisseur's expression of confident eagerness. Her eyes lit when he stood naked before her.

He proved her hungers and her experience. She knew all the womanly tricks. She also enveloped him, engulfed him, holding him tightly in her strong arms against the cushion of her fragrant breasts, taking from him what she needed. Halliday had known many women along the border and deep within Mexico, but never one quite like Kate. He forgot time, forgot where he was.

Later he lay in a hazy stupor, drowned in the softness of the big bed, nearly sure that he would never rise again. Kate had left him to turn out the light, and now she was back at his side, relaxed, her even breathing telling that sleep had come. He was aroused by a man's voice coming from a distance, shouting, hoarse in its authority.

"Sam, Sam, you heathen, where are you? Come here and open the gate."

Kate Wormack sat up in bed, and even in the darkness Halliday sensed her rising fright.

"It's Pierson. Texas, wake up. You've got to get out of here."

"I'm awake."

But Halliday was still groggy with sleep. He sat up, shaking his head, a bawdy laughter within him that Pierson, for all his reputation, had been unable to satisfy this woman.

"Hurry," Kate said.

He said: "To hell with Pierson. He doesn't own the world."

92

Her voice was bitter, rueful. "That's what you think. Get out of here. Go out the back way while you have time. He'll kill you if he finds you here. He might even kill me."

This last, he saw, was her major concern. But her fear was real enough to stir Halliday to haste. He rolled out of bed, fumbled for the clothes he had dropped on the floor. Below, through the open window, he could hear Pierson still bawling for Sam to open up. It was obvious that the outlaw had been drinking, and the question now in Halliday's mind was: *How drunk was the man?*

He pulled on his pants, his boots, wriggled into his shirt, then fumbled through the dark for his gun and could not find it. Only then did he recall that he had removed his belt before supper, had hung it across the back of the patio chair. He cursed under his breath. With his gun, he was not afraid of Gabe Pierson or any man. Without it, he felt naked and helpless.

He pulled the door open and stepped out into the balcony in time to see Sam's shadow scuttle across the stone-paved square and unbolt the gate. A full moon floated high in the sky, lighting the patio as if it were a stage. Halliday saw a blocky man lunge through the gate and catch the frightened Sam by the front of his loose shirt.

The shouting voice came: "What took you so long? Where's he at?"

Sam gibbered in pidgin English, so frightened that Halliday could not make out a word. Neither, apparently, could Pierson. He flung the small figure from him. The cook stumbled backward, crashed into a table, went down in a heap. Pierson started for the stairs.

Halliday knew that he had to get down those steps before Pierson reached their bottom. They were the only way from the balcony. He ran. He had covered half the steps when

Pierson's foot touched the lowest one.

The outlaw froze. His big hand was poised over the butt of his holstered gun.

Halliday launched himself in a leap, his hurtling body flying directly down at the man below. His knees, drawn up, caught Gabe Pierson in the chest as the gun came alive. Halliday's impact knocked the weapon from Pierson's hand. It arched across the patio to land close to the unconscious Sam. Pierson sprawled on the patio floor.

Halliday fell on top of him. Pierson rolled clear, came to his knees, then up to his feet with the sureness of a cat. Halliday rose with him and they faced each other like two stylized wrestlers, big bodies bent forward, hands spread and extended, ready for an opening. Pierson lunged, trying to wrap his ape-like arms about Halliday. Halliday side-stepped the rush and chopped viciously at the side of a thick neck. The blow dropped Pierson to his knees. Before he could come up, Halliday kicked him heavily on the jaw. The kick should have put Pierson out. It did not. He shook his head twice, then surged up and stood swaying.

But the liquor clouds had been knocked out of him. His native craftiness had taken over. He was abruptly alert and cautious. He struck out of perfect motionlessness with a looping right that caught Halliday, split his cheek above the high bone, and made his head ring. Pierson had a lot of power and knew how to put the full weight of his body behind a blow. They sparred, each respecting the other. They were both taking punishment, pounding at each other with all the skill they possessed. Pierson threw a right. Halliday took it on his forearm and moved in.

Pierson hooked a left that cracked against Halliday's chin. Halliday went down and Pierson aimed a kick at his head. Halliday caught the booted foot and dumped Pierson hard. They were both sucking for air, fighting for breath as they regained their feet. Pierson was an instant slower, and, as he rose, his jaw was exposed. Halliday swung at it, knowing that—in his doubly spent condition—if he missed he could not muster another effective blow. But his knuckles connected squarely, and the big outlaw sat down, stayed in a sitting position for a long moment, then quietly settled on his back.

Halliday stood over him. His knees shook and his face was a raw mask, dripping blood. His breath whistled as his lungs labored for oxygen. Then, slowly, walking with extreme care like a man gone too far in alcohol, he crossed the patio, took his gun belt from the chair, and fitted it carefully about his hips. He lifted the heavy weapon and spun the cylinder to make sure it was free. He dropped it back into the holster, then dropped himself into the chair, resting his arm on the table.

He stared at the unmoving figure. This was the man from whom he had intended to buy horses. He cursed himself, thinking that now he would never make the deal. He had not only licked Gabe Pierson—he had also made free with Pierson's woman.

He glanced up and saw Kate standing at the balcony rail, looking down at him. She wore a wrapper and her dark hair floated loosely about her shoulders. She stood quietly for a long moment. Without a sound she turned, went back into her room, and closed the door.

A scraping noise came from behind Halliday. He spun around. Sam had sat up. He groaned, said something incomprehensible to Halliday, rose painfully to his feet, and padded toward the kitchen without looking at Halliday.

Halliday knew that he should go—but where? He had come for horses, and all the horses seemed to belong to

Gabe Pierson. He could get his own mount and ride out to meet the incoming herd, but, if Pierson were angry enough when he came to, he would likely gather his friends and ride after Halliday. Better to wait, to face the beaten man alone.

He sat in a kind of stupor, unaware of how much time passed, letting his body recover from the battering. He watched vacantly until Pierson stirred. Halliday's mind felt detached. *Maybe I should shoot him and be done with it. He wouldn't be missed by many. I might even take over his men. . . .* But Halliday's hand made no move toward his gun. He saw Pierson roll. The outlaw spotted Halliday and managed to heave himself to his feet.

"You licked me." There was no anger in the voice, only some wonder, as though Pierson were making a statement he could not quite believe. He tried again. "You licked me."

Halliday stood up. "I licked you."

"What do you know?" Pierson shook his head. "I never got licked before. It must have been the way you heaved off those stairs that kind of threw me off."

"Probably," said Halliday.

"You're all right." Pierson seemed to become engrossed with the cuts and blood on Halliday's face. "I marked you up some."

Halliday said honestly: "You damn' near killed me."

"So?" The words appeared to please the outlaw. "Seems we've each met a man. Come on, let's buy a drink."

Halliday knew that he probably should not ask the question, but he wanted things straightened out before he left the patio. "What about Kate?"

Pierson blinked at him. "What about her?"

"I didn't know she was your woman."

"Hell," said Pierson, reaching out and catching his arm.

96

"What's a woman between friends? Damn, we're likely the two best men in all California."

He led his new friend through the gate, and neither looked back to where Kate was watching them through a crack in the window curtains.

VI

Halliday drove eight fresh horses to the cañon mouth and headed uphill, beside the tumbling waters of the Kern. His face was swollen and bore the marks of the fight. His muscles ached, but he had had four hours of sleep in the livery barn and his possession of the horses heartened him. Gabe Pierson had not protested the price. Pierson seemed to believe that Halliday was one of the great people.

Halliday had spent some riding time speculating on the peculiarities of the outlaw's mind. Apparently the only value Pierson accepted was force. He had sold the animals far below their true market price because Halliday had licked him in a fight.

An hour past noon Halliday saw his point rider come around the bend above him. The first of the cattle followed. Halliday studied them as they lumbered toward him. The water had helped, but the steers were still gaunted to skin and bones. As soon as the drive reached the flats and grass, he would have to stop for a day or two and let them graze.

He waved and drove the horses into a side draw to let the cattle go past him. The herd moved slowly, the many hoofs stirring the rocky soil into a dust envelope that cut most of the animals from view. He watched, wondering where María was. He was surprised at his eagerness to see her. He found no sign of her as the riders passed down the trail. At last, Norton, riding drag, appeared out of the dust and pushed to his partner's side.

He looked at Halliday's marked face without surprise. "Have any luck? Get any horses?"

"Eight." Halliday nodded at the draw. "They're probably wet-branded, but we can't afford to be choosers. Where's María?"

Norton evidenced interest in Halliday's state of health instead of answering. "What happened to you? Have to fight the fellow to get the horses?"

"Ran into a gent named Pierson . . . Gabe Pierson. He didn't like the attention I was giving his girl."

"Pierson? Gabe's in Bakersfield?"

"That's right. You know him?"

"Used to, down on the border. A rough customer. So, he licked you."

"I licked him."

Norton was incredulous. "You licked Gabe Pierson in a fight?"

"I did and he liked me for it. Where's María?"

Norton wet his lips nervously. "She ain't here."

"What do you mean? Where in hell is she?"

"I guess she's headed back to the mission."

Halliday's hand snaked out and jerked Norton's horse closer. Only inches separated the two men. "What did you do to her? So help me if you did something to hurt or scare her out . . . I'll eat your heart."

"Hold up." Norton tried to pull his horse away. "Listen before you go off half cocked. I didn't have a thing to do with her leaving. There were too many of them . . . and Hahn promised that, if I gave them trouble, they'd stampede the herd for the hell of it.."

"Who's Hahn?"

"Whitey Hahn, a mean *hombre* with white hair and kind of pinkish eyes. Foreman of Gunlock. He had six of the toughest brush jumpers I ever saw . . . gunmen. He'd been sent to take the girl back to the mission and warn the *padre* to keep her there."

"Make sense, man. Who sent him?"

Halliday released the other's animal. Norton backed his horse a few steps.

"Bruce Alban, her uncle. Seems the mission people sent a messenger to the ranch to tell him the girl had left with you. The messenger made better time than we did, with the herd, and Alban rousted out Whitey to take her back."

"How long ago did they leave here?"

Worry jumped into Norton's voice. "Look, Dan, there's six of them and they're rough customers. You couldn't get her away from them."

"How long?"

"Well, two, three hours. But. . . ."

Halliday cut him short. "Drive the cattle on down to the flat and hold them on the grass until I get back." He swung his horse and headed back uphill toward the pass.

It was full dark before he crossed the summit, and his main fear was that Whitey Hahn and his men would press on to the mission without stopping to camp. He did not know how he could take the girl out of the mission again if the *padre* opposed him.

An hour after he turned down across the divide, he saw a pinpoint of light wink far down the cañon, marking the location of their camp. He slowed his horse to a walk and moved forward with extreme care. He did not expect Bruce

100

Alban's men to have guards out. They would have sized up Norton and his sorry outfit and would not expect any challenge from them.

He rode to within a quarter of a mile of the fire, found a brush-filled draw, and tied his animal there. He climbed the rock wall and worked along it until he was above the circle of light. Then he squatted down to watch. It was no part of his plan to attack as long as most of the crew were awake. He could not handle six gunmen. And he did not want María killed in a fight.

María, too, was watching. She sat at one side of the blaze, her eyes filled with a burning hatred for the men her uncle had sent after her. She did not want to go back to the mission. She knew that the *padre* would listen to her uncle against her, and that she could never again hope to escape. She found herself wishing that Dan Halliday were here, although she had no idea what Halliday could do against this crew. These men were professionals and too many for any single man to handle. She could see no help—unless she managed to help herself. The thought seemed hopeless until it brought her the glimmering of an idea.

She had seen how these gunmen had looked at her as they took her in tow, had sensed the increasing tension she caused among them. She was deathly afraid of Whitey Hahn. She had known him at the ranch before Alban sent her to the mission. She had concluded that he was an inhuman being, not moved by the emotions that softened other men. He had a streak of sadism, a love of seeing men or animals writhe in pain. She had seen him beat a horse, seen him enjoy cutting one of the Mexican riders to shreds with a bullwhip—and she had no doubt that he would coldly kill her if her uncle so ordered. Nor was she fully convinced that the order had not been given. Her death would ease Bruce Alban's takeover of the Gunlock. Her aunt was her only close relative and would inherit from her.

Then she had another thought. She was married now. That made a difference. If she died, the title to Gunlock would go to her husband. She felt safer in the realization. Alban would not want her dead until he could do something about Dan Halliday. He would prefer her locked up at the mission. Without her presence, the Spanish-speaking *vaqueros* who had ridden for Mike Mulrooney would not follow Halliday, and he would lack the manpower to take the ranch away from her uncle.

She knew with certainty that she must not allow Whitey Hahn to take her to the mission. Somehow she must slip away, work back over the Tehachapi and down to Bakersfield. She must try to catch up with Halliday and urge him to find gun hands in the outlaw town to support him in a fight for the ranch.

But she could not hope to escape alone. She studied the men around her, one by one, knowing that each one around the fire, with the exception of Hahn, was covertly watching her. She met the eyes of one and smiled and, after the passage of some minutes, favored another with the same smile. She had learned much from her night with Halliday. And before that she had known she possessed something men wanted—often craved more than gold—something they would cheat, lie, and murder for.

The fire burned low. One man and then another rolled into his blanket and went to sleep.

Whitey came to stand above her and say: "Go to sleep." His voice was flat, without feeling. He did not actually care whether she slept or not.

Without speaking to him she took her blanket and withdrew to a little hollow, where a rock partially hid her from the camp. She curled there, huddling, pretending to sleep, but actually following Hahn's movements through half-closed eyes.

Hahn went to one of the crew who had not yet retired. "You'd better take the watch, Bailey. Wake Jordan at twelve. We'll ride at four."

Her heart pounded with hope. Bailey was one of three men at whom she had smiled, a slender gunman whose face was lined despite his youth. His eyes were habitually insolent and restless below a shock of tow-colored hair.

She waited. Whitey stretched on the hard ground and lay quietly. Bailey, carrying his rifle in the crook of his arm, went out to check the picketed horses, then came back and walked silently to her rock and peered down at her.

She said softly: "I'm not asleep."

He jumped as if the warmth of her voice had gone through him with a shock.

"I'm thirsty. Could I have some water?"

He unhooked the canteen from his belt, dropped to his knees, and put the canteen into her hand. She made sure that in taking it her fingers brushed his. She took a long swallow, tipping up her head, showing her long throat. She fastened the cap and handed back the canteen, stretching her bare arm and again touching his hand.

He started to rise, but her fingers closed over his wrist.

"Don't go. I'm frightened."

He glanced toward the figures sleeping around the fire, looked back at the girl. "What are you afraid of?"

"Of going back to the mission . . . of what they'll do to me there. I've got to get away."

He started up again. Her arm slid around his neck and tightened, bringing his head down until her lips found his. The kiss became long, lingering. She could sense the fire she lit in him. Probably in all his miserable life he had never seen a woman as desirable as this girl. Those he had known in the saloons were painted, blowsy, and aging.

"Help me." Her lips were still against his. "Help me and you'll never be sorry as long as you live."

Suddenly Bailey was seven feet tall. "How?"

"Saddle two horses. Walk them as far from camp as you can. I'll stay here and watch. If anyone stirs, I'll whistle."

"Where do you want to go?"

"Back into the hills. We'll wait there a few days . . . until my husband gets to the ranch."

"Your husband?"

She kissed him again. "Don't let that bother you. I'll manage."

He believed her because he wanted to. He was not the first man to be tricked by a woman, nor would he be the last, María guessed.

When she released him, he straightened, saying: "I'll be back when the horses are. . . ."

He did not finish the sentence. Whitey Hahn made a noise behind him. Whitey stood close, a gun in his hand.

"Drop the rifle, Bailey."

His tone was low but a deadly quality in his voice made Bailey blanch. Bailey let the rifle drop. He knew Whitey, expected at the next moment that the revolver would explode and send a bullet crashing into his chest.

"Hahn, listen. . . ."

No shot cut him short. Suddenly Halliday stood behind Hahn, his gun jammed hard into the foreman's ribs. "Take it easy, Hahn."

Hahn stood as motionless as stone. He did not know who was behind him, but he understood the feel of the gun barrel. He let go of his own revolver and heard it *clink* onto the rocky ground.

Halliday said to María: "Pick up both guns and get the revolver from him." He nodded toward Bailey.

Bailey made no effort to resist. He seemed surprised to find himself alive. From Whitey's tone he had known that he was a dead man.

Halliday considered him. "I'm Dan Halliday," he said. He took Bailey's revolver from María, who came to stand beside him. "I'm the husband she told you about. She stands to own Gunlock now that we're married. You know . . ."—he spoke slowly—"that they're going to kill you as soon as we ride away."

Bailey knew it. All hunger to fight had been squeezed out of him. He nodded.

"All right. I can use you." Halliday flipped the man's revolver back to him. "But I'll be watching you. Pull that trigger against me and I'll gut shoot you. Side with me and you'll be paid Gunlock wages. And no bullets in the back."

Bailey glanced pure hatred at Hahn, turned to Halliday. "It's a deal." He holstered his gun.

Halliday said: "Gather up all the guns you can find in camp. And you,"—he pointed his revolver at Hahn—"stretch out on the ground and reach your hands as far above your head as you can."

Hahn's inward seething showed in his hot eyes. He lay down, and Halliday handed his rifle to María.

"If he so much as wiggles an ear, blow him in two," Halliday told his wife.

Her dark eyes sparkled in the moonlight. "I knew you'd come," she said, putting a rich feeling into her voice.

He did not comment. He had witnessed her whole act with Bailey. He swung away, strode toward the fire where

Bailey was quietly collecting guns.

"Find a sack for them."

One of the sleepers stirred. Halliday was at his side in two quick steps. He brought his gun down against the man's skull. It made a popping sound. The man groaned once, lay still. Halliday did not know or care whether he was dead. A second man moved, and Halliday knocked him out. Then they were all awake, grunting as they sat up. Halliday swung his gun to cover the group.

He said in a tight voice: "Stay where you are unless you want your heads shot off."

His language was one they understood. They sat alert but still.

Halliday told Bailey: "Go saddle two horses, one for yourself, one for my wife. Tie the rest together on a lead and bring them here."

Bailey smiled thinly. "What if I ran out?"

"You'd have both Whitey Hahn and me after you."

Bailey nodded thoughtfully, moved away. Halliday paid him no more attention. Bailey would string along.

While Bailey was bringing the horses, Halliday tossed more wood on the fire for added light. Then, watching the crew, he went for Whitey Hahn and brought him down to the camp under his short gun. María stood guard as Halliday tied the mouth of the sack that held the crew's rifles and revolvers.

"You won't be needing these."

Hahn shouted angrily: "You going to leave us afoot and unarmed in these hills?"

"Makes sense. I've got trouble enough without worrying about your trailing me."

"You'll have trouble when we catch up with you."

Halliday said: "Bailey, take their boots. They won't be

so fast barefoot in the rocks."

Hahn fell silent.

Halliday considered him for a moment, then said to Bailey: "Never mind." He motioned to Bailey to lead the horses out and walked María back to where he had left his own mount. They continued up the trail, Bailey out front where Halliday could watch him and María at his side.

When they had crossed the crest, Halliday hid the gun sack deep among the rocks and returned to his wife to find her eyes on him.

She said: "This much is true . . . I never in my life was so glad to see anyone."

A hard smile touched his lips. "I listened to you con Bailey in that same tone."

She was quick to anger. "What was I supposed to do, just let them haul me back and lock me up forever in the mission? I didn't know there was any help within miles."

"I guess you did what you had to do," he conceded. But he remained disturbed by her facility with the man.

They rode steadily through the night, not speaking again. It was afternoon when they caught up with the herd, now clear of the cañon mouth and spreading out across the welcome grass.

VII

Norton listened to his partner with a frown. When Dan finished his story, Norton swore in rising annoyance.

"Damn it. We're not clear of them hardcases. That Hahn is tough."

"We won't have to worry for a couple of days. He's only got three healthy men with him now. I don't know about the two I buffaloed, but I hit them pretty hard."

"Sure. And what have we got to fight with when they get horses and hardware and come to settle the score? Hahn isn't going to forget . . . and he knows you're handicapped with the herd."

"Well, we've got Bailey to help."

Norton shook his head. "Bailey's gone . . . rode out half an hour ago. Said he'd seen all of this part of the country he wanted to. He don't like the idea of what Hahn would do to him, in case we lost."

Halliday looked out over the grazing cattle, weighing their needs and his chances. The animals should have at least a week before they hit the trail across the flat valley where the temperature often held at a blistering 120°. "We need help."

Norton stared at him. "Just where do you think you're going to find it out here?"

"What about your friend, Pierson? He likes a fight."

"He also likes to get paid. We're close to broke."

María stood listening but taking no part in the talk. Now she said with more assurance than she had shown since her rescue: "I'll pay him as soon as I'm in possession of my ranch."

Dan Halliday and Norton both noted the personal pronoun, and exchanged glances.

"We'll need gun hands until I can reach the *vaqueros*," she said. "Where is this Pierson."

"Bakersfield," Halliday answered.

"That's not far. Ride in with me and we'll make a deal with him."

Dan Halliday flushed. He saw Norton's knowing smile and it angered him. He knew what his partner was thinking. María was already taking over. He nodded to her. "Let's go," he said, and went to pick up fresh horses.

Norton looked coldly at the girl. "Don't push him too far."

She flashed him a quick smile. Now that she was back in the comparative safety of this company her natural self-assurance was restored. "Don't worry, Cap. I'll handle things."

Norton frowned as she walked proudly away.

Halliday and María rode into Bakersfield's main street and reined in before the livery well after dark. The old hostler eyed Halliday with unmasked surprise.

"You're getting to be a regular, mister."

Holliday grinned at him. "Gabe Pierson still in town?"

"Far as I know."

"At the Fremont?"

"Where else?"

"You'd better stay here," Halliday told his wife. "I'll go see Pierson."

"Why?"

"The Fremont is a saloon."

She said: "Mike used to take me into saloons."

"You were a little girl then. Besides, the Fremont is different."

"Different how?"

"Well, they have girls there to drink with the men and. . . ."

She patted his arm like a mother reproving a dull child. "Dan, I was raised among men at the ranch. I know what is done in that kind of place, and I'm not afraid to see it."

The hostler was listening and the knowledge made Halliday angry again. He took her arm and steered her up the sidewalk at a pace too fast for her comfort.

Gabe Pierson stood at the end of the bar with Kate Wormack. He saw Halliday in the doorway, and let out a shout in his bull voice. "Hell, look who's back! The only gopher that ever licked Gabe Pierson. Come over here, you shorthorn, and we'll see can we drink this joint dry."

María had come in under Halliday's arm as he held the louvered door wide for her. Pierson stared in open shock. Every man in the room turned to look. Pierson came forward slowly, pulling off his black hat and rolling it in his big hands.

Halliday said: "This is my wife, María. Gabe Pierson. Man I told you about."

She smiled. It seemed to Halliday that she could not resist flirting with every man she met. She said: "I'd heard a good deal about you before."

"I'll bet." Pierson's wide mouth split in a proud grin. "Did your man tell you he licked me?"

"He did. It's hard to believe."

"You're Mike Mulrooney's girl, ain't you?"

"Yes."

"Mike, the old son-of-a-bitch, came near hanging me last time I saw him. Seems I was riding a horse he thought was his."

"Was it?"

Pierson's grin spread and his eyes twinkled. "Never did find out. I was too busy hightailing." He turned to Halliday, his face sobering. "You hadn't ought to bring her in here."

"I tried to keep her out. She's got a mind of her own."

"Bet she has. Any Mulrooney's got one. Old Mike was as opinionated a man as I ever knew."

Kate Wormack swaggered forward, a nasty twist to her lips and speculation in her eyes. Halliday was afraid of what she might say, but he saw no way to keep the two women apart.

"Welcome back to Bakersfield." Kate looked directly at Dan, then smiled at the girl. "I suppose this is your first visit to a place like this? Don't let it frighten you."

María returned the smile, but her expression lacked the warmth it held for men. "Mike used to take me to saloons. I'm not here to embarrass you. We came on business." She looked at Pierson and the touch of charm returned to her face, her voice. "We'd like to talk with you."

"Why not?"

María nodded to the saloon woman and turned toward the door, missing the slow wink Kate sent across to Halliday. The three walked toward the livery and again it was María who took the lead.

"My uncle is holding my ranch," she said. "And now that I'm married he has no right to do so."

Pierson grunted, indicating that conditions at Gunlock

were an open secret throughout that section of country.

María went on: "So, we're taking our herd"—Halliday noted that she had already assumed ownership of his half of his and Cap's animals—"to the Santa Marguerita. But we don't have a fighting crew, and Whitey Hahn has more than twenty men riding for my uncle. Do you know Hahn?"

Pierson's expression became withdrawn. "I know him." Plainly he was not committing himself until he knew what the game was and what the stakes would be.

"We need men who know guns to stand against them. So we've come to you," María said as if she might have been inviting Pierson to a party.

"Ah? And what would you be considering paying my men?"

She did not hesitate. "We haven't any money. But the Gunlock cattle are in the best of shape. The steers should be worth fifteen to twenty dollars a head at market. If you'll bring a crew to match my uncle's, I'll give you five hundred steers as soon as I hold the ranch."

Halliday's breath whistled. The offer was better than $6,000 for a few days' riding. He glanced at Pierson and saw a certain tightness around the outlaw's mouth.

María said: "You can split the money among your crew any way you choose."

Pierson laughed suddenly. "It's a deal, ma'am. Where's the herd?"

Halliday told him. "We want to hold them on the grass for a few days, put a little tallow on their ribs, before we throw them across the valley."

Gabe Pierson extended his hand not to Halliday but to María. They shook solemnly.

The gesture rankled in Halliday, and, as he and María rode out of town, he said sourly: "You've kind of got the bit

112

in your teeth, haven't you? Norton warned me you'd try to run the show."

She looked at him quickly, then pushed her horse so close to his that she could reach across and put a small hand over his. "That was the only way to do it, Dan. After all, I own the ranch. Pierson wouldn't have believed you as easily as he believed me."

Halliday was not satisfied, but he hid his feelings as they pressed on. They found the herd scattered for nearly a mile along the river. The riders circled them idly, although there was little danger that they would stray far.

Norton greeted Dan with acid humor. "She make your deal?"

Halliday kept his displeasure out of his tone. "Pierson will be out here tomorrow with twenty hands. They ought to be enough to handle the problem. You haven't seen anything of Hahn and his hikers, have you?"

His partner showed a brief, bitter smile. "They're probably still walking. And they're going to be burned up. No rider cottons to being afoot . . . I just hope we don't have trouble with Pierson."

María stared at him, surprised. "I thought he was your friend."

Norton shrugged. "With a friend like Gabe, a man don't need enemies."

Dan Halliday kept watch that night. He did not believe the stranded Gunlock crew could have found horses and arms so soon, but he could not be sure. And having come this far, he wanted to take no chances. He rode slowly, circling the herd. They had bedded down quietly, thankful for the water, the grass, and for the fact that they were not called upon to plod wearily over the mountain trail.

Halliday's mind reached out to the future. He was beginning to recognize that María had not compromised her independence by marrying him—she might well want to be rid of him once he put her in control of her inheritance. His mouth set tightly. If she thought she could push him aside, she had another think coming. Dan Halliday was not easily pushed. He had taken care of himself from the time he had first climbed a horse.

The adventure of the Mojave ranch had seemed a gateway to a bright future, but at their best the few bleak acres he and Norton had left were nothing beside the Gunlock. Gunlock in the right hands could be as it had been under Mike Mulrooney, one of the great ranches of central California—no better grazing land could be found anywhere. Dan Halliday meant to have Gunlock, meant to hold it even against his wife.

Gabe Pierson rode into camp late the next morning.

With his coming, any danger from Whitey Hahn was past, and three days later Dan started the herd moving westward across the wide sweep of the flatland that was the lower end of the great valley.

The three days had been wearing on Halliday. Gabe Pierson made no secret of his interest in María, and she seemed thoroughly to enjoy the outlaw's company. They were together much of the time, riding around the herd, pushing their horses through the brakes along the river. The crew watched, Norton watched—and Dan Halliday suffered the growing knowledge that they were laughing at him.

On the second afternoon he caught up his wife's horse, and told her curtly: "I want to talk to you."

She looked at the stony mask of his face and made no protest. She followed him. He led her down and across the river, then up a rocky draw that wound back toward the rim of the hills. Not until they were a good four miles up the main cañon did he turn into a small box cut and step to the ground.

"Get down."

She dismounted slowly. She was wary, unusually uncertain. She asked: "What's the matter?"

He trailed the reins so that the horses could graze on the scant, dry bunch grass. He took her shoulders and forced her to look up into his face. "Do you have to ask me? What are you trying to do to Gabe Pierson?"

She said as lightly as she could: "Oh, that." But he could see that she was frightened, that she sensed the depth of his anger and read in his stormy face the wall he had built against her charms. "Don't be foolish, Dan." She knew better than to let her own anger show. "We need him if we ever hope to take the ranch."

"And after we take it, what then?"

"We get rid of him."

"María," he tried to speak quietly, as if he were explaining to a child, "you haven't had much experience with people like Pierson. That man is as deadly as a rattlesnake. He smiles. He's pleasant. But all his life he has taken anything he wanted. I don't know how many men he has killed in the taking . . . I doubt he's bothered to keep track. In his book human life is the cheapest thing there is."

"He's not going to kill me."

"If it served his purpose, he wouldn't hesitate. But he probably would think himself better served by killing me."

"Are you afraid of him?"

Dan shook his head. "Not the way you mean. I whipped him once. The next time he comes for me, it will be with a gun . . . and I'm not afraid of that, either. I think I can

115

outgun him, and he knows it. A man like Gabe can tell how you feel. What I'm wondering is how we get rid of him. You promised him five hundred head of cattle. When he sees the thousands on the Gunlock range, he's not going to be content with a measly five hundred head. He'll take what he wants."

"You're forgetting my *vaqueros*. They number more than a hundred, and they'd die for me . . . each and every one of them. When the time comes, I'll have Gabe Pierson hung to an oak tree if he gives me any trouble."

He stood speechless. It was incredible that the scared girl he had taken from the mission had developed so positive a self-confidence in so few days. She was truly Mike Mulrooney's daughter. But his own position in her plans remained unstated.

"And what about me?"

Her eyes widened. "What do you mean?"

"Will you use your *vaqueros* to run me off, like you intend to run Pierson off?"

"Why Dan. . . ." Tears actually welled in her eyes. "How can you say so cruel a thing?"

His hands tightened on her shoulders. "Because of the way you're acting."

She said steadily: "I'm doing what I think has to be done. Once we're on the ranch, things will be different. Now kiss me and stop acting like a fool."

She lifted her full lips, red and inviting. In spite of his intent, hunger for her raced through Halliday. His hands slid from her shoulders, behind her, and drew her slender body to him. Her lips were warm and open. They seemed to drain the life from him as the kiss held. His hands slipped down over her hips and he started to loosen her clothes.

She tried to pull away, but his strength held her easily.

116

"Dan, please. . . ." Her mouth moved against his. "Not here."

"Why? There's no one within miles." He was undressing her, and after a moment she sighed, realizing that she had no way to stop him.

Her body was quiet beneath him for long moments. Then, as if he had lit a spark, she flamed to life, twisting to meet him, fighting yet yielding, her fingers digging into his shoulder muscles with the desperation of her need. When it was over, when they lay side-by-side on the dry grass, the sun warm on their bare bodies, Dan Halliday knew a resurgence of the confidence that had been waning through the last few days. She was his. He could control her, take her, do as he willed with her whenever he chose.

VIII

The town of Gunlock was as much a part of the ranch as
was the big adobe house standing at the head of the single
street. The community was built around a plaza, an open
square of sun-dried earth dominated by the church, the
hotel, the livery stable, and the ranch office from which
Bruce Alban ran the huge operation. The buildings were
adobe brick, built of the very soil on which they rested and
plastered with the same stuff, all earth and earth color. The
quiet sleepiness of the place made Halliday restless.

He, María, and a half a dozen of Gabe Pierson's riders
had pressed on ahead of the herd.

Bruce Alban was not unwarned. Whitey Hahn and what
remained of his crew had ridden in the day before. Foot-
sore, sullen, angered at their ordeal, they had circled past
the slow cattle, had reached Bakersfield, rearmed, and
learned there that Pierson and his men were with Halliday.
Thus when the Halliday troop came in, grouping before the
hotel and the next-door livery corral, Bruce Alban stepped
from his office across the street and greeted his niece.

He was still a handsome man, although nearing sixty.
And he still looked more the gambler he had once been
than the prosperous rancher. He wore a black broadcloth

suit, despite the heat, a wide-brimmed, low-crowned hat, a white shirt, and black string tie.

"Welcome home, my dear." His voice was hearty. He sounded pleased. "Your aunt has your room pretty and ready for you at the house."

María stared at him in utter astonishment. She hated this man with a loathing for which she could not find words. That he could even pretend pleasure at seeing her—after what he had done to her—left her feeling that the ground had dropped from beneath her.

Halliday, seeing the look on her face, said without emphasis: "No need. We'll go to the hotel until you can vacate the house."

Bruce Alban's eyes changed. It was the only sign of emotion in his gambler's face. "And who might you be?"

"María's husband."

Halliday looked at him squarely. Alban knew who he was. Halliday had seen Whitey Hahn behind the window of the ranch office.

Alban said: "So you're Halliday. But as far as the marriage is concerned . . . there's some question about its legality."

Halliday asked flatly: "What question?"

"María is a minor. I am her guardian, and I did not give my consent. By what I have heard from the *padre,* you practically kidnapped her, told him you had Mike's blessing."

Halliday waited, saying nothing.

"Virginia, my wife, tells me you were at the ranch only once, that you barely saw María who was a child at the time . . . you certainly were not intimate enough with Mike for him to promise his daughter to you."

Halliday lowered his head like a fighting bull. "We're married. The *padre* can tell you that."

Alban shook his head. He had not stopped smiling. "It's not quite that simple, friend. You obviously overcame a weak-willed, inexperienced girl. I don't know what enticements you used. We'll let the court decide."

Halliday said dryly: "It won't work, Alban. We're married and there is nothing you can do about it."

Alban's white teeth flashed. "Young man, I'm afraid you are a better cattleman than you are a lawyer. We have several possible courses. We can go before the court and explain that my niece has the mind of a child, that she has shown an inordinate interest in men, even at an early age, and that we placed her at the mission for her own protection. We will point out further that she is heiress to a very large ranch and you're little more than a brush-jumper, that you took advantage of her simplicity and her overdeveloped appetite for sex to try to cheat her of her inheritance."

"All outrageous lies." The words came on María's indrawn breath.

Her uncle raised an admonishing hand. "Don't get so excited, my dear. We have witnesses to your conduct before you went to the mission, when you tried to run away with one of the hands."

Halliday caught Gabe Pierson's eyes and found mockery there. His impulse was to tell Pierson and his men to take Alban, throw him bodily off the Gunlock, or get rid of him in any way they chose. Caution made him examine the street and he saw men on the roofs of all the buildings around the plaza, sunlight glinting off their rifles. He was nicely in a trap. He put down his sudden rage, and said quietly: "I've got two thousand steers a couple of miles back. They need graze and water."

"Why, of course." Alban's voice was smooth. "You can

throw them along Center Creek. I'll have one of my boys show your crew."

"Take care of it, will you," Halliday told Pierson. "And leave a couple of men to cover the doors of that hotel. We don't want to be bothered."

Pierson grinned knowingly, beckoned to two of his riders, and, with them, followed Alban's guide back to meet the oncoming herd.

Silent, Halliday and María led their horses to the livery, and afterward entered the dark, narrow lobby of the hotel. Not until he had signed the register, received a key from a fat, soft-looking Mexican, and had followed the girl to the room and locked the door securely did Halliday speak.

Then he said in a whisper: "Looks as if we rode into something."

She was red with anger. "How does he dare call me weak-minded, say I'm man crazy? The only man who ever forced me. . . ."

"Quiet down," he said, thinking of the thinness of the walls.

"I won't!" she raged at him. "I married you to get away from the mission, and I slept with you to keep you on my side and take back my ranch . . . and now what? He'll get a court order annulling the marriage. I'll be right back where I was . . . but worse off. He'll put a lifetime brand on me, ship me off to the mission, and go on running Gunlock just as if he owned it."

Halliday was angry in turn. "I don't mean a thing to you, do I?"

She was too furious to dissemble now. "Why should you . . . a ragged-ass gunman rancher with a clutch of starving cattle? What do you think Mike Mulrooney's daughter will settle·for in a man?"

His own temper was still up from his meeting with Alban and her naked assessment enraged him more. "All right," he said. "It suits me to be free of you. I'll pull out. Maybe Gabe Pierson can do more for you."

At once she was alarmed. "You can't do that. You can't abandon me now . . . for that bastard to do what he wants with. You said you'd get me the ranch. You said all you wanted was pasture until your place got water. You made a deal. Does Dan Halliday go back on his word?"

And he was trapped. He had always prided himself on his word—the last pride he had. She had called him a gunman—but his skill with guns he had always hated and feared a little. He said roughly: "Where is the judge who will hold the hearing?"

"Santa Marguerita."

"Who is he? Maybe I'd better go talk to him."

"That won't do any good. He's been in Alban's pay since Mike died."

Dan Halliday had had few experiences with the law. Most of his life had been spent along the border where legal authority was scarce or nonexistent. He abandoned hope on finding justice on his side here. "All right," he said grimly. "We'll use Gabe's people to take the ranch . . . and we'll have a gun battle on our hands they'll hear in San Francisco."

María said: "If we can hold on until I can talk to the *vaqueros,* we'll have an army that'll run Whitey Hahn right over the rim of hell. Then let the judge do whatever he wants. There won't be enough people in the county to take Gunlock away from me."

Once more she had used a possessive pronoun in a way that shut him out of her future. He pulled back into himself, prowled to the narrow window, and stared out at the town, fuming.

A knock rattled the door and he swung around, his hand instinctively dropping to his holster. In this town lived no friends—every man was another's potential enemy. He pulled his gun and glanced at his wife. Her eyes were on the door, wide with fright.

He whispered: "Don't worry. No one's going to take you away." He crossed the room on silent feet, the gun ready in his right hand. He used his left to open the panel.

A small Spanish woman stood outside. She seemed old, at least sixty. Her face was lined. Her eyes stared dully. At sight of the gun she cringed back.

María called in surprise from behind him. "Juanita!"

The woman came out of her terror. She brushed past Halliday and folded María in her arms. The two women stood together sobbing, head to head, while Halliday checked the hall to see if anyone else was there.

He came back in and shut the door. "What's the matter now?"

Her arms still wrapped around the old woman, María said: "This is Juanita, the nurse who raised me."

"Why the tears?"

"We're happy to see each other."

Halliday stared, dropped the gun into its holster, and sat down tiredly on the bed.

The woman's weeping diminished and was replaced by a torrent of Spanish. Halliday knew enough of the language to make himself understood in the drinking places along the border, but now he heard a different accent and he could not follow what was being said. But he soon saw that Juanita's words were horrifying María.

He asked: "What is it?"

"The worst news yet." María was pale. "Alban has driven all the *vaqueros* off the ranch."

Emptiness touched the pit of his stomach. He had counted on these men. "Where did they go?"

"Back into the hills. They've built themselves some shacks, but they're starving. Most of them were born on the ranch . . . and so were their fathers before them. They haven't anything. Most of the houses in town are empty."

"Does she know where to find them?"

Another rapid exchange of Spanish ensued.

María said: "She'll get word to her cousin, who will call the leaders together where I can talk to them."

"When?"

Again the exchange.

"Tomorrow," María told him. "Maybe the day after . . . or the day after that."

Halliday groaned. "*Mañana*. That's the Spanish word for never." Then he said urgently: "Tell her to get them as quickly as she can. Make it clear to her that you're in danger . . . she must move fast."

María translated the message for Juanita, listened again, and translated for Halliday. "She understands. She has heard the house servants talking about my uncle's plans. He may try to put me into an institution." Her voice broke. "Can he do that?"

"I don't know. Would it help if you talked to your aunt?"

She gave a bitter laugh. "You don't know Aunt Virginia. She hasn't a brain in her pretty head, and she thinks Bruce Alban is a king who stepped down from his throne to marry her. He's told her a silly story about being related to royalty and that he came to this country to hide because people next in line were trying to assassinate him."

"Doesn't she know he was a gambler?"

"He claims he gambled to save his life . . . to disguise himself. What I told you about his raping me is true. Aunt

Virginia doesn't suspect a thing. He's a total liar and smooth as silk."

"He'll trip himself up some time."

She sounded despondent. "I doubt it. His kind always seems to come out on top. Let's go stay with the herd . . . I'll feel safer there."

"You're safe here," he assured her. "With Gabe's guards at the doors and with me in here. No one is going to get past me to hurt you . . . and if Alban owns the law, he'll work through the courts. Why shouldn't he?"

She was not as confident, but she agreed to stay.

She and Halliday ate in the hotel dining room without incident—unless the fact that they were the only guests could be construed as ominous. But the only person to come near them was a Spanish girl, who waited on them and who did not recognize María.

Halliday was bone weary. He had gone without sleep for three nights, watching the herd, watching Gabe Pierson's men. The bed, when he and María were again in their room, felt more than welcome. It was not as large or as soft as Kate Wormack's bed, but he did not care. He was asleep as soon as he stretched out.

María lay in the deepening darkness, her fears growing around her like a shroud. Finally, near midnight, she could control them no longer. This morning everything had seemed within her reach. She would have her ranch. She had felt secure with Gabe Pierson's guns behind her. She would be María Mulrooney again, mistress of Gunlock, with a hundred *vaqueros* obeying her every wish as if she were a feudal princess. Alban would be dispossessed.

Now all her morning dreams had collapsed and she felt dangerously vulnerable. She lay in the hot night, naked to the stifling air, her husband breathing heavily beside her.

The fact that he could sleep added to her distress and anger—yet she needed him at this moment as she had never needed anyone in her life.

"Dan," she shook him. "Dan, wake up."

He awoke completely in an instant—tonight the instinct for survival that had kept him alive through many troubled and gun-fast years was especially keen. His hand went beneath his pillow for the gun there and he sat up, trying to see in the blackness of the little room.

"What's wrong?"

"Hold me."

"Hold you?" He stared in the direction of her voice. "Why?"

"Just hold me. I'm scared. Make love to me, kiss me, and make me forget."

Making love to her had been in his mind from the moment he and María had entered the room. Still, he was ashamed of his instant's suspicion of her. Bitterness was in his tone. "I thought you didn't want me. I thought our marriage was just a business deal."

She was crying suddenly in the darkness. "Don't think of what I've said. Just make love to me."

Her soft hands reached for him, and, in spite of his angry feelings, he felt himself come to life. He bent to kiss her. "It's all right," he said gruffly. "Night isn't a time to think. Shadows grow into monsters."

He put his gun away, lay down again, and for long, thoughtless minutes made her lose her fears and doubts in the strength of his embrace.

Finally she slept, curled into a soft ball in his arms. Halliday fell into a heavy, dreamless sleep after daylight had grayed the window. It seemed to him that he was awakened again almost at once, by a pounding on the door. His fingers searched for the gun.

"Who is it?"

"Cap. Open up."

"What's the matter?"

"There's hell to pay. They stampeded the herd last night."

María had sat up. Halliday pushed her down and threw a light blanket over her nakedness. He pulled on his pants and unbolted the door. Norton charged in, paying no attention to the girl in the bed. He was shaking with anger.

"They hit us just after midnight. None of us expected trouble, and the two nighthawk riders didn't know what was happening until the first shots went off."

Halliday said: "Settle down. How many riders?"

"How in hell do I know? It was dark and the damn' cattle came charging right through our camp. A steer stepped on my chest. The wagon's gone. The camp's wrecked. And those doggies are scattered from hell to breakfast. I rode out with Gabe at first light. They did a real good job. Our stock is so mixed with Gunlock beef that it would take a full roundup to cut them out. When are María's Mexicans going to show up? The only way we'll get our herd back is to take over the whole ranch."

IX

The camp was a total wreck. The chuck wagon was up-ended. Its bows were broken. Its canvas cover was trampled and ripped to shreds. The cook who had been sleeping beneath it was dead.

Dan Halliday surveyed the scene while what remained of his crew and Gabe Pierson's men gathered around, waiting for orders. Halliday had none to give. He had no idea of what immediate course to take. Separating his cattle from Gunlock's would be an impossible job. Cutting out 2,000 head of starving steers, wild as antelope on the first good grass they had seen in months would be like trying to round up a bunch of deer. Alban had won time to press his threat to have María's marriage annulled. Halliday and Norton would lose everything they had worked three years to accumulate if Alban won in court.

Halliday's impulse was toward murder. He wanted to ride back into town, stride into Alban's office, and kill the man with his fists. But he knew that Hahn's gunslingers would be standing by, eager for a move by him. He would never get within hitting distance of Alban.

María sat her horse as if dazed. She had been struck wordless. Halliday imagined her thoughts ran in some vengeful track parallel with his.

Norton spread his hands in anger. "Well, what do we do about it?"

María straightened, sparked by the words. "We take the ranch. We'll have to do it quickly . . . before my uncle can have my marriage set aside."

Halliday looked up at her. "And how do you propose to take it?" he asked.

She made an impatient gesture with her hand, indicating Pierson. "He's got enough men to run Alban and Hahn out of the country."

Halliday was not convinced that her estimate of Pierson's strength was accurate, but of one thing he was sure. If Pierson won control of Gunlock before he and María could round up her *vaqueros*—María, Norton, and he would be at the mercy of the outlaw and probably as badly off as they were now.

Pierson said: "The ante goes up." He was speaking to the girl, not to Halliday.

She asked: "Ante?"

"You offered us five hundred head to help drive the herd and put it safely on the ranch. We did." He grinned. "Now you want more done. You want your uncle and Hahn run out or killed. Right? So, the price goes up. You're in a bind, ma'am, a tight one . . . and I'll be glad to help because you're a pretty girl. But the world is full of pretty women, and I'd get a little thin helping them all unless I got paid."

She said reluctantly: "How much do you want?"

"Well." He sounded as if he were thinking through a knotty problem. "You haven't got any cash, in fact, we might say you haven't got anything, unless I get it for you. That right?"

She nodded.

"So maybe I should have half."

"Half? You're crazy!" Halliday was raging. "Do you know how much Gunlock is worth?"

"Oh, I wasn't thinking of the ranch," Pierson's voice was oily. "I wouldn't dream of asking for half the ranch. It would tie me down and I'm kind of fiddle-footed. No, I was only talking about the cattle."

"You're still crazy. There must be ten thousand head."

"And how many have you got? Not one. You haven't got the ranch, either. And when Alban gets to that judge, you may not even have a wife. Seems to me that a man like you, sitting in a game with a busted flush, is being kind of particular." He turned his back to Halliday, looked at María. "What about it, ma'am?"

She was torn by indecision. It told in her face.

Halliday said quickly: "I want to talk to you alone, María."

Pierson made no objection. He smiled mockingly at the man he had so recently called his friend. Right now he was a gambler who held every card in the deck.

The girl hesitated, then let Halliday lead her horse beyond the ruin of the chuck wagon. Her mouth was set in a stubborn line when he spoke.

"Don't make a deal with him yet."

"Why not? What have I got to lose?"

"Everything."

She shrugged. "He only wants half the cattle. I'll still have a fair herd . . . and I'll have the ranch. None of us has anything without him."

"Wait. Stall him. Juanita is getting in touch with the Mexican riders. With them behind us, we won't need Pierson."

Her lip curled. "And while we're waiting for them, Alban

will have seen the judge and I'll be on my way to the mission. No. I'll use the force we have at hand." She pulled the rein free of his fingers and cantered back to where Pierson waited.

Halliday stayed where he was, looking after her in helpless anger.

Norton rode to him. "Don't be a jackass, Dan. Go along with us."

Halliday's head came up sharply. "Us?"

Norton flushed and his tone became quarrelsome. "Us. I'm throwing in with Pierson. What else can I do? Our steers are lost, unless he takes the ranch. You'd better come in with us, or you're going to wind up with nothing at all, and maybe dead. It could be Alban will figure the easiest way to get his niece unmarried is to forget the judge and just let a sniper take you out of his way."

"I'll watch."

"So you'll watch. What else do you think you can do?"

Halliday decided that now was the time for him to keep his own counsel. He no longer trusted Norton. "Maybe I'll drift."

Norton snorted. "Are you crazy enough to ride away from all this?"

"From all what?" Halliday asked. "If Pierson wins his play, he'll be the one in control of Gunlock."

"He only wants half the cattle."

"You believe that? Did you ever see a hog get one hoof into a trough and not push in all the way? Pierson wants all the cattle, the ranch, my wife."

"From the looks of things you might be better off without her. We haven't had a stroke of luck since you pulled her away from that mission."

Halliday almost hit Norton. But fighting with Cap

would do no good. He walked to his horse, swung into the saddle, and, without troubling to look back, headed for Gunlock.

The town drowsed in the morning sun. A group of men around the ranch office eyed Halliday with detached but total attention. They had dismounted. Their horses stood at the rail. Halliday sensed that they had been expecting him. But a glance told him that Whitey Hahn was not among those in sight, nor was Bruce Alban. He turned across the plaza to step down and enter the hotel.

The same fat Mexican was behind the counter.

"You know Juanita?" Halliday asked.

"The maid, *si*. She back there." He tipped a thumb toward the hall.

Halliday moved back along the dim corridor. The doors of several rooms stood open. He found the old woman making the bed in the third room. He went to her, and asked: "Did you reach your cousin?"

Her black eyes questioned him uncertainly. "María?"

"They are watching her." He did not say who was watching.

The old nurse bobbed her head. "I talk to Pedro, Pedro Ortega. You know the creek that runs down to the river beside town?"

"I crossed it coming in."

"Follow creek to the river. Pedro will be there. But don't let anyone see you go."

He thanked her and left the hotel, feeling the eyes of the group across the plaza on him as he mounted. He did not return their attention. He half expected them to stop him from leaving town, but no one moved from the shade patch under the spreading live oak. Still, he took no chances. He

132

crossed the creek and continued toward the wrecked camp until he crested the brow of a low hill. From there, he could see that his back trail was clear. He swung his horse to the left and rode toward the Santa Marguerita. He did not follow the creek, figuring that, once he reached the river, he could turn westward until he found the junction. The terrain permitted him to watch better his back trail. He rode at a steady pace, marveling at the grass that here grew high enough to brush his horse's belly. It was a cattleman's dream country, as lush as any he had ever seen.

He rode up a sharp rise into a clump of oak and there dismounted. He made sure his horse was hidden among the trees, bellied down on the crest, his gaze covering the trail over which he had just ridden. He watched for nearly an hour. The only movement he saw was a knot of grazing cattle far to his right.

Satisfied that he had not been followed, he rode down to the river. It took him another hour to see the silver stream twisting through the flanking growth of tules and tightly bunched willows. He turned downstream, still watchful. But the land seemed empty, its rolling hills and grassy sweep broken only by park-like live oak clusters that dotted the slopes.

He pressed on to the river's junction with the creek. He expected to find his man waiting on the bank. He saw no one. Nor did he find tracks. Puzzled, he hid his horse in the heavy streamside growth, had a drink of the crystal clear water, and sat down with his back against a tree. The sound of running water was soft, friendly, soothing.

Trouble seemed distant in this Eden. He fought off dozing. The angle of the sun changed and told him that he had been at the rendezvous a full two hours, and the worry beset him that there had been a hitch, that Pedro Ortega was not coming. Then sound behind him alerted him and he twisted his head.

A man stood within five feet of him. That he had come so close without Halliday's hearing his approach gave Halliday a chill. He must have been daydreaming, nearly asleep.

The man was not young. He wore a conical hat of straw, a cotton shirt, and pants. His bare feet were thrust into homemade *huaraches*. But he wore a revolver in the belt around his slim waist and carried a rifle cradled in the crook of his arm.

Halliday said: "Pedro Ortega?"

"Yes. You are María's husband?" His English was good but had the soft, musical tones of Spanish.

Halliday nodded.

"Where is she?"

"She couldn't come," he lied. "She is watched."

He saw the shadow come into Ortega's liquid eyes and knew that the man did not trust him. He damned María for not having come. Aloud he said: "Her uncle won't let her out of his sight and we didn't want to make him suspicious."

The reference to Alban made Ortega's face tight. Hate glittered in his eyes. "Dog."

"Dog he is," Halliday agreed. "María wept when she heard how he has used her people. She wants you to come out of the hills, to come back home to Gunlock."

"I have been watching you for two hours to make sure you came alone," Pedro said. "Or that others would not meet you."

"I'm alone."

"I know. Come."

Pedro waited for Halliday to mount, then splashed

134

through the shallow water, climbed the rise on the far side, and found his animal in the trees there. He led northward toward the rising hills. The country changed. The soil turned thin and rocky, the growth diminished, and scrub pine appeared. The grass was short and brown—useless. It was hardscrabble, land so poor that Mike Mulrooney had not wanted it added to Gunlock. It was into these sorry hills that the *vaqueros* had retreated, bewildered at being driven from the ranch, too accustomed to obeying orders to be able to act positively on their own.

Well after dark, Halliday and his guide rode into the yard of a *ranchita,* a small place, and Pedro sent his call through the night. The house showed no light and no dog had barked a greeting, but now a lamp was lit within and the door was opened.

Shadows came across the dark yard. A man took the horses in silence, and Pedro led Halliday through a doorway he had to duck to pass into a low-ceilinged room. Then he was facing the leaders of the *vaquero* exiles.

They sat on the earth floor, their backs against the adobe wall. The furniture in the room consisted of a pile of blankets as a bed in one corner, a wooden bench, and homemade table. The men sat wearing their conical hats, their shoulders wrapped in serapes. The temperature in the hills dropped as soon as the sun went down. The evening was chill.

Pedro introduced Halliday simply as María's husband.

An old man, who they called Sanchez, did the talking for the group. The rest sat stoically, silent as Indians, only their dark eyes moving to tell their interest.

Halliday told them the story of Alban's sending María to the mission and of keeping her there. He explained that, under her father's will, she had inherited the ranch when she married, and that he and his wife had come to take possession of her ranch.

"But Alban wants to trick her out of it," he went on. "He is trying to have the marriage annulled, send her to the mission for life, and keep control of Gunlock."

He saw that they did not understand—to them marriage in the Church was binding. Most of these men had not troubled with that formality, had taken their wives in common law, but the idea that anyone could cancel that union, once a priest had heard the marriage vows and blessed the union, was beyond their comprehension. They lifted their shoulders and looked at one another, suspecting him.

He tried a different tack.

"Do you want to go home, back to your old houses, where you will have plenty of beef, beans, and chili?" He saw by their eyes that they did. "Then ride with me. The ranch belongs to my wife, and I mean to take it for her. But I need help."

He did not tell them about Gabe Pierson and his crew.

Old Sanchez asked slowly: "How many men do you have?"

"You are my men, María's men. You ran the ranch when Mike Mulrooney was alive. You will run it again."

"What about the wolf . . . Whitey Hahn . . . and his fighting dogs?"

Impatience rose through Halliday.

"They're fighters, of course. If they weren't, we would not need help."

"Our people are not fighters in the way these men are."

"You're telling me you're afraid?"

The old man was patient. "I'm saying that we are peaceful. Only under the *patrón*, Mike Mulrooney, did we fight well. That is why Alban could drive us away."

"I will lead you as Mike did . . . to fight for María, the *patrón*'s daughter."

"Let her come to us," Sanchez advised. "Let her explain her need. Then we will see."

Their suspicion of him was deep. He guessed they feared that what he proposed was some new trick of Alban's, a way to tempt them out of the safety of their barren hills and destroy them.

"All right," he said, "I'll bring her here. Will you ride if she asks you to?"

"We will see."

It was the best answer he could get from Sanchez, and he knew that, if he pressed them further, he would only deepen their distrust of him.

The meeting was over. Like shadows the men vanished one by one into the dark yard. Ortega's wife brought out cold beans and made tortillas before the open fire, baking them on the hot bricks. A girl came in, Ortega's daughter, about María's age. Her face was smooth, oval, deep-toned, and her straight black hair gave off a luminous shine.

Her father said: "This is Dolores." And to her: "This is the new *patrón*."

Halliday wondered if Ortega actually accepted him as head of the ranch or if the words were mockery. But he saw no guile in the face. He bowed to the girl. He ate the beans and hot chiles, the sour sweet tortillas she brought him. They did not apologize for the food and refused to eat until he had finished. They gave him goat's milk to drink, and afterward he pulled out his sack of tobacco. He saw the *vaquero*'s eyes glisten and held the tobacco and papers toward him.

Ortega rolled his cigarette ceremoniously. He drew in the first lungful of smoke as though starved for the taste, fondled the sack for a moment, then offered it back.

Halliday waved it away. He could do without a smoke for a few days. A sack of tobacco was a cheap price for a friend.

Later they insisted that he take the bed. They retreated to share the stable with the horse and two goats. He stretched out on the blankets, feeling the weariness of the past days, hearing the rustle of the dry grass tick beneath him. He lay wondering where María was now, whether Gabe Pierson had already moved against the ranch. He was nearly asleep when the slab door creaked on its leather hinges.

He came up on one elbow. "Who is it?"

"Dolores," said the soft voice. "Do not be afraid, *señor*."

He could see her against the lighter square of the doorway. She lifted the thin dress over her head, and he saw a shapely young figure. He had a horrifying picture of Ortega with his rifle, trailing his daughter across the yard and catching her like this. He had trouble enough without being chased by an outraged Mexican father.

"Go away, quickly." His whisper was urgent.

She padded barefoot across the baked earth floor and sank to her knees at his side.

He knew that she understood English.

"Go away."

"Why, *señor*? Do you not like Dolores?"

"I like you fine. But I'm married to María."

"Yes. But you are the *patrón*, no? The old *patrón* was married, but he gave himself to all of the girls. He was not stingy."

Halliday's sudden impulse was to howl with laughter. He stifled the spasm with difficulty.

"You don't understand. I love María."

"That is good. I understand. She is *patrona*, she also understands."

Halliday sweated. He had never before been in this situation.

He said desperately: "Dolores, I am your father's guest, his friend. I could not betray his trust."

"Oh? It is Papa you worry about? But it is Papa who told me to come. He says, go and keep the *patrón* warm on this cold night."

She bent over him and kissed him without warning. She knew the art well. Her lips were hot and parted, and the tip of her strong tongue thrust around, caressing his.

Involuntarily he reached, drew her against him. Whatever scruples he had had dissolved under her ardor. This was not an inexperienced girl—as María had been. Dolores knew every gesture, every method of pleasing a man.

When she had exhausted him and sighed her contentment, he whispered against her cheek: "Somewhere you learned."

Her mouth turned against his and her voice was drowsy. "I was married to a *mucho hombre*. He was killed two years ago. I have waited long, long time for this night."

It was still early, barely daylight, when Halliday rode out of the hills behind his guide, Ortega. Whether Dolores had told the truth about her father's having sent her to his bed, Halliday did not learn. He could tell nothing from the *vaquero*'s manner. They traveled several miles in silence.

At last Halliday asked: "Do you think that, if María comes to them, your people will ride with us?"

Ortega's face was unreadable. "I cannot say, *señor*. Perhaps."

Halliday had a sense of drowning in "perhaps" and *"mañana"*. But nothing he could do would hasten the decision. He studied the trail, giving attention to the landmarks and turns, and, when Ortega pulled up on the hill above the river, he was confident that he could return without a guide.

He raised his hand in salute, rode down to the stream, and splashed across the shallow ford. He headed for the camp where he had last seen María. He was not sure of finding her there—or Norton or Pierson. They might have already descended on the ranch and taken it. But he did not want to risk going into the town alone again, and he doubted that Pierson had made his move.

Alban and Whitey Hahn would be watching for a retaliation for stampeding the herd. They would be ready. Gabe Pierson was too old a hand to ride into a hornet's nest. His style would be to lie doggo, to catch a few riders at a time away from the headquarters and dispose of them, to weaken Hahn's force until he thought he had an undisputed advantage before he struck directly.

His guess proved correct. The chuck wagon had been righted and the crew was at its evening meal. They looked up as he rode in.

Pierson said with irony: "Light and chow up, stranger."

Halliday dropped out of the saddle, pulled it off the horse, and turned the animal into the rope corral that had been strung between four oaks. He came to the fire.

One of Pierson's men had taken the post of the dead cook. He dished up a plate of boiled beans and beef. Halliday noted the meat. It was too fat to have come from one of his trail cows. He squatted with the plate at Pierson's side.

"Alban send you your supper?"

Pierson's grin was pleased. "Critter walked right in and asked to be ate."

"Heard anything from Alban?"

"Nary a word." He waved toward a line of low hills not far away. "Couple of his boys laid up on that ridge this afternoon and watched us make over the camp."

"Where'd you get the beans?"

"Gunlock. Sent half a dozen riders in for two measly sacks. No trouble."

Halliday cleaned his plate, avoiding the eyes of his wife,

who sat across the fire, watching him. He gave no indication that he was aware of her being there.

"What are your plans?" he asked Pierson.

"Thought Norton said you were pulling out."

Halliday looked at his wife. "Maybe I thought of something better." He saw interest flare in her eyes. Again he spoke to Pierson. "How do you mean to earn all those cows?"

Pierson chuckled. "That's what Alban's wondering . . . and that's the way I want it. I half expected he'd send a bunch to order us off the ranch. So far he hasn't . . . but I can just see him stewing. And sooner or later his crew will have to quit town and start working cattle. That's when we'll give them trouble. Time's on our side."

"You'll run out of grub."

"Sent a pair of boys back to Bakersfield this morning. They'll bring up a wagonload. We'll make out until they get here." He yawned enormously, scratched himself, and spat into the fire. "Me, I'm turning in."

As Pierson stood up, Halliday asked: "Where's Cap?"

"Out with some others, scouting around. If we can catch enough cattle close to town, we might run three, four hundred down the main street just to give friend Alban something to chew on. I believe in never letting a man rest easy when he's given me trouble."

Pierson moved away toward his blankets, and one by one the riders sought theirs until Halliday was left alone with María across the dying fire.

In a whisper that he could read on her lips rather than hear, she asked: "What better way did you think of?"

He stood up and went to stand above her, shaking his head. "You'd only tell Pierson."

"What makes you say that?"

"You're siding with him now."

"I'm not." Her voice came up a little in anger. "It's just that he's all the chance I have."

"I talked to Ortega."

She was surprised. "Where?"

"At his house back in the mountains. I talked to him and Sanchez and a few others of your father's *vaqueros*."

"What did they say?"

"They want their homes back. But I'm a stranger, so they don't trust me. They said they'd listen to you."

She sighed, shook her head. "I can't leave here."

"Why not?"

"Pierson won't let me. He says I'm his ace. He wants me where I can give him a bill of sale when he's ready to claim the cattle."

"He's taking all of them now?"

"Are you back on that subject again? No . . . not all. He gets half. I keep half. And I don't give him the bill of sale until we have the ranch. But he's being careful that I'm here to sign it. I heard him tell the man on guard not to let me out of his sight."

"If I can get you away . . . will you go to the *vaqueros?*"

"I can't afford to."

"What does that mean?"

"Gabe Pierson will pull out and not make the fight."

"You don't read Pierson very well. With all this beef on the Gunlock range, you couldn't drag him away from here with an ox team. Go turn in and pretend to sleep. I'll take care of the guard and saddle the horses. When I whistle, come running."

She could not make up her mind.

He drew her to her feet and held her shoulders, looking at her intently. "Believe in me, María."

"Well. . . ."

She turned reluctantly and went to her blankets at the other end of the camp, well away from the men.

He waited ten minutes, then rose, took a cup, and moved to the coffee pot that simmered at the edge of the glowing coals. He filled it, wandered toward the guard sitting on a rock from which he could oversee the whole camp.

"Coffee?"

The man was startled.

"I'll trade it for a cigarette. I lost my tobacco."

"A deal." The man took the cup and set it on the ground, found his sack and papers and handed them over.

Halliday rolled his smoke and returned the makings. The guard did what Halliday hoped he would, cupped a paper, shook the yellow flakes into it, rolled it, then dropped his head to lick the seam.

Halliday's hand rested on the butt of his gun. He drew it and brought the heavy barrel down on the crown of the guard's head. The man fell off the rock without a sound and lay still in the grass.

XI

Riding through the night toward the shallow cañon of the Santa Marguerita, Dan Halliday was buoyed up by the sharp awareness that this was his and María's ranch. It would be his to develop if he could defeat Alban and Pierson. He never doubted that.

His mind was busy planning projects. He wanted to dam the river, put in alfalfa for winter feed, separate the young stock from the ranch animals, and bring in better bulls to upgrade the herds. He could add perhaps 100 pounds of meat to each beef. The cattle on the range were descendants of the original cattle brought up from Mexico by the Spaniards when they colonized this portion of the state—and while they were heavier than the infamous Texas longhorns, who walked off weight faster than they put it on, they were no match for the crossbred Herefords now beginning to appear on the plains of Kansas and Nebraska.

His wife said testily: "What are you so deep in?"

He realized that he had not spoken to her for over an hour. "The ranch," he said quickly.

"What about it?"

"Making plans."

"Don't forget whose ranch it is."

145

His annoyance came strongly through his voice. "You don't really give me much chance to forget."

He drove his spurs into his horse's flanks and the startled animal leaped ahead, taking him at a full run down the bank, through the willows, and into the water of the ford. On the far side he pulled up and waited for María.

"We'll ride into the hills and camp," he said quietly. "I've an idea it wouldn't be too healthy to come on Ortega in the dark. I get the idea that those people are pretty edgy . . . they might shoot first and ask questions afterward."

She was sulking and did not answer.

He led the way across the rim of the cañon and on into the broken hills. He found a side draw sheltered by a clump of oak that broke the wind. He swung down, pulled his saddle, and hobbled the horse. Without speaking to her, he cared for María's animal, then spread the blankets in a soft depression, shed his boots and pants, and rolled into his blanket, still in ill humor.

María lay alone, staring sleeplessly through the great branches of the oak, through the dripping veils of Spanish moss at the stars that seemed to bloom in the tree. She was angry with herself.

What's the matter with me? Why do I always pick a fight with him? She thought about it intently for the first time. *It's the ranch. I want Gunlock and I know he wants it, too. He wants it more than he wants me . . . that's the trouble. He'll try to dominate me in order to dominate the ranch. . . .* Now, she was actually facing the problem, she thought. *I've got to make him want me more than anything else. If I don't, I'll lose everything. . . .*

She threw back the blanket and rose. Halliday did not stir although she sensed that he was not asleep. She went to him, carrying the blanket.

"Dan, I'm sorry. A devil seems to get into me."

He said without turning: "Go to sleep."

"I'm cold."

She pulled his blanket from his shoulders, spread it, lay down, and threw her cover over them both. He did not pull away, but neither did he touch her. He lay on his back, immobile as a log. She had expected him to turn to her. She waited. When he still made no move, she unfastened his shirt buttons and ran her hand lightly over the swell of his chest. He did not unbend, but she felt him tense.

Presently he groaned, a man driven. He rolled. His hands found her shoulders, ran down, and caught the fine flare of her hips against him. His mouth sought hers and his lips pressed hard, devouring hers. Suddenly they were clamped in a close embrace.

"María. María." His whisper was a confrontation. "Why do you fight me when I'm trying to help?"

She could not answer. The breath for talking could not be spared from her effort to achieve what she desired until the surge of a dam bursting told him her reaction was complete. She moaned and dug her nails into his flesh.

"Hold me . . . hold me . . . hold me. Just don't say anything for a little while."

He held her. She wept against his chest.

"Dan, I don't know what I'd do without you, I don't . . . I don't know."

He said: "It's all right, María. You won't have to do without me . . . the choice will always be yours."

She felt closer to him than ever before. She slept.

They took the trail before full light, without breakfast. María led the way—she had known these hills intimately since her childhood. When they halted on a small rise to let

147

the horses blow, she looked at Halliday. She seemed disturbed.

"What do you think Pierson will do when he finds I'm gone?"

"Probably hang around and try to pick up the cattle you promised him. Let's push."

In the afternoon, they crested a sharp hill and looked down on the little Ortega *ranchita*. They rode down to the yard. Large-eyed children stared at them, then ran like frightened quail to spread the alarm. Two women came immediately from the adobe, one of them Dolores. Halliday knew instant concern about how she would greet him. How would María react to a too friendly Dolores?

He saw Ortega in the dark doorway of a shed, a rifle held waist high. As María and Halliday dismounted, Ortega came forward. He removed his straw hat and bowed low to María. Halliday realized he had no need to be nervous about Dolores. She seemed cowed by María.

Ortega was saying: "Welcome, *señora*. We have little . . . but what we have is yours."

María received his homage with a warm smile. She and Halliday were escorted into the house. Nothing but amenities were exchanged until she and Halliday had eaten.

At last María said: "I've come to you, my people, to ask help."

A shadow clouded the smile in Ortega's eyes.

"*Señora* . . . I do not know."

"What do you not know, Pedro?"

"The *vaqueros* are afraid. *Sí*, that is bad. It is sad. But the Alban and Hahn are wicked men who have brought evil to all of us."

María gestured regally. "The more reason you should rise with me and destroy them."

Ortega seemed unhappy to be arguing with the daughter of the Gunlock. He shrugged helplessly. "It is not I who say no, *señora*. It is some of the others that do. I will ride today. But what can three of us do against Hahn . . . and against the renegade Americans who have come to the ranch?"

"What do you know about other Americans?" Halliday asked.

Ortega threw him an accusing glance. "We keep watch. Nothing happens on the Gunlock that we do not know."

Halliday recognized his mistake in not mentioning Pierson before. A few Mexicans—like Juanita and the hotel clerk—still worked in the town and undoubtedly kept track of the obvious events, relating the information to their relatives in the hills.

He tried to remedy his error by ignoring it and turning the accusation back against Ortega. "When I came to you alone, your people promised to ride if the *señora* herself asked you. Have you changed your minds? Are you not men?"

The old man drew himself up with dignity. "I said I myself would ride. About the others, I said we will see."

"Then bring them here and let the *señora* talk to them."

"Perhaps they will not come."

María said at once: "Then we will go to them. Pedro, you will guide us."

The old man bowed his head, then turned to go to his stable. María turned her eyes from the old man and smiled at Dolores, the mother, and the silent, watching younger children.

"It will be all right. Times will be good again," she assured them.

She beckoned to Halliday, and went to her horse.

Halliday's eyes met Dolores's dark gaze. A smile

stretched her full lips, her first change of expression since they had ridden in. He looked away. He read both remembrance and promise in that warm glance and secretive smile, and something in him responded. He would have to be very careful. He could not afford to become involved here.

When they were mounted again, in a fierce undertone, María hissed: "You said that if I came, they would go with us. Now we're worse off than before. I've run away from Pierson . . . and what chance do we have with neither him nor the *vaqueros?*"

"You give in too easily," he said. "Isn't there any fight in you?"

He was angry again. In a minute he and María would be spitting at each other like cats.

Ortega's arrival next to them kept her from answering. They followed Ortega to the first small house, although they hung back from him about ten lengths.

At last María said thoughtfully: "Maybe it's better this way. If we talked to them all in a group they'd have the strength to refuse me . . . but individually I doubt that they'll turn me down."

XII

Gabe Pierson rose as first light paled the eastern sky. He moved to the fire and became annoyed when he found white ashes and the coffee pot cold. He looked toward the rock where the guard should be sitting, the man who should have kept a blaze alive, and did not see him.

"Harper, where the hell are you?"

He received no answer from the guard but his racket roused the camp. Men tumbled from their blankets, reaching for their guns. Cap Norton came running, fastening his cartridge belt as he ran.

"What's happened?"

Pierson said: "I don't know. That damn' Harper let the fire go out and I don't know where he is."

A yell from the rock turned them around.

"Here's Harper! With his head bashed in."

Pierson and Norton ran clumsily in high-heeled boots.

"Is he dead?"

The rider who had found the guard was kneeling, his ear against the man's chest.

"He's still breathing, no credit to whoever hit him."

Pierson whirled. "Where's the girl? Where's Halliday?" He strode to the spot where María's blanket had been.

Norton headed for the corral and came back, calling ahead: "Their horses are gone!"

Pierson fell to cursing. "I'd ought to have killed Halliday in Bakersfield. I should have shot him when he rode back in last night."

"Better think about what we're going to do now," Norton advised.

Pierson calmed instantly. "Why, we'll do what we planned in the first place. Ride into Gunlock and take over. Then we'll round up the cattle. And we won't settle for half this time . . . we'll take the works."

The crew had come up to listen.

Norton said in a dry voice: "You haven't got the girl to give you a bill of sale."

"We can rig one." Pierson smiled. "Don't worry about it. I know cattle buyers in Bakersfield who won't ask questions. But we can't have her showing up to spoil the deal." He looked over the crew, choosing two men. "Joyce, you and Turner pick up their trail. It shouldn't be too hard to follow. Find Halliday and his wife and make sure they don't come out of the hills. The rest of you rustle up some grub. Then we head for Gunlock."

An hour later they strung out on the trail a mile short of town. Pierson split the party. He put the second group of men under Cap Norton's command. "You circle around and come in from the south. Keep out of sight, behind that range of hills, until you hear me shoot. Then ride in fast."

Norton nodded, wheeled his group away. Pierson gave them half an hour's start. Theirs was the longer distance.

Pierson looked over his contingent, sixteen of the hardest cases in the valley. He had total respect for Whitey Hahn and Bruce Alban. His orders were terse and sure.

"We want Hahn and Alban first," he explained. "The

rest of that crew will fold. They're riding for money. Hahn and Alban want what we want . . . big names and power. Don't start the shooting until I say. We'll drift in, straggle out to cover the street from all angles." He paused, gestured to one of his men. "Younger, you ride with me. You and I will go to the ranch office. If Alban isn't there, we'll have to go up to the house. Fast. I don't know where Whitey'll be . . . we'll have to play for him the way the game breaks. Alban's our ace when we get him. All right, let's ride. When we sell those cows, there'll be better than a thousand dollars for every one of you."

He grinned at their faces. Not a man in this crowd would hesitate to murder for a twentieth of that sum. They hit the saddles happily, spread out casually into singles or twos, and headed to Gunlock.

At noon they came quietly into the main street, turned their horses into the hitch rails. They dismounted, pretended business in town or squatted in the shade of the adobe houses that lined the way. They positioned themselves unobtrusively to cover the full length of the dusty street, giving no indication of the violence to come.

Gabe Pierson and Clyde Younger walked their horses through the town and swung down before Alban's office. Several of the ranch riders loafed on the sidewalk. Pierson nodded civilly and went into the office. Younger followed him through the doorway, pausing as he stepped inside and saw that Alban was alone in the square room. Younger turned around, putting his back to Alban. He stood in the shelter of the doorway, watching the street.

Alban looked up from his desk. He smiled at Pierson but his voice had an edge. "It's about time you and your crew pulled out, Pierson."

Gabe Pierson returned the smile. His tone was conversa-

153

tional. "That's what I came to see you about. Your niece promised me half the cattle on the range for helping her get her home."

Bruce Alban opened his mouth, but for an instant he said nothing. Then he kicked back his chair and rose to his feet. "You're lying or you're crazy. You don't expect me to let you ride off with half my cattle?"

Pierson still smiled. "*Her* cattle. And a bargain's a bargain. We don't leave until we're paid."

"Then you'll rot on Gunlock." Alban raised his voice. "Henry, Joe, get . . . !"

The words vanished in a gun blast. Pierson's gun had leaped into his hand. His shot took Alban between the eyes.

Clyde Younger's gun began to hammer in the doorway before Alban fell forward across the desk. Three of the men outside went down, their guns half drawn. Two fled for cover, firing as they ran. Pierson's men, hunkered along the street ahead of them, cut them down. No casual observer could have told who fired the last shots before the street was quiet again.

Whitey Hahn was visiting his girl in a house at the lower end of town. He heard the shots and rushed into the street, without his shirt, a heavy gun in each hand. He saw Clyde Younger step out of the office. Hahn paused and pulled down. The shot was long for a revolver, but Hahn's first bullet drilled Younger through the heart. Several shots from the street answered him, but missed. He raced to his horse, leaped into saddle, and boiled out of town.

As Hahn crested a rise, he saw riders galloping toward him. For an instant he thought the men were the balance of his crew, attracted from the ranch by the shots. He realized his mistake when a bullet sang over his head. He jerked his horse around and tried to outrun his attackers. He looked behind him. The newcomers had wheeled into his trail and his pursuers from town were fanning out.

He struck out for the rough mountains beyond the Santa Marguerita. His fleeing horse put a foot into a gopher hole and snapped its right front leg. The fall threw him headlong. He landed hard on one shoulder, the impact knocking the wind out of him. He lay gasping but the drum of pounding hoofs spurred him to rise. He stood, legs spread, facing the crescent of riders pouring down upon him. He recognized Cap Norton and recognized death. He had been in too many fights to expect any mercy at Pierson's hands.

A great, burning rage filled him. He ran to his struggling horse, jerked the rifle from its saddle boot, and bellied down behind a rock pile. His first shot dropped a horse. His second knocked a man from the saddle.

The onslaught veered away, circled out of range. Hahn held his fire. These men respected him as a fighter, but he had no real hope. Darkness that would let him escape was hours away. He discounted the possibility that his crew would come to his rescue as a remote chance. A few of his men would be at the ranch bunkhouses or around the blacksmith shop but a number were on the range.

The sun beat down, burning into his bare back. He would be dangerously blistered before evening. His thirst grew and the shoulder on which he had landed ached.

Time ran on.

He lay watching the Pierson riders. They had bunched on the hillside just out of rifle range and seemed to be holding a conference. He wondered if he could surrender—but he knew he was too big to ride for Pierson. The man would receive him with a smile and shoot him in the back. Better to hang on as long as he could and take as many of his attackers with him as possible. He checked the shells in his belt. He had more than enough ammunition to kill them all if he had the chance. He wondered briefly about what had happened to Bruce Alban, then put his whole attention again on the enemy.

Pierson's group moved, breaking into two parts and beginning a wide circle. The tactic reminded him of an Indian fight he had once been in over in Arizona Territory. He and three friends had forted up in some old mine buildings with twenty or thirty savages crawling through the rocks, trying to get at them. He had not expected to live then—but this was not a fair comparison. No cavalry detail would show up now to help.

The afternoon sun brought him dizziness as well as thirst. The besiegers were out of sight except for an occasional figure skulking through the rocks. He waited for a clear shot. His mind played tricks. He had the delusion that the enemy had gone and started to stand up. A bullet kicked up rock chips close to his head. He dropped and searched for the spot from which the shot had come and found the wisp of muzzle smoke. It was a long way off, but it did command his position and in a moment of clarity he knew that, sooner or later, the gun would find him.

He scrambled around his rock pile and immediately drew fire from the other side. Then he knew that the last of his hope was gone. He pulled down his pants, tore a piece from his underdrawers, tied it around his rifle barrel, and waved it as high as he could in the air.

At once a horseman came around a clump of brush. Gabe Pierson's voice reached Hahn. "Had enough? Come out with your hands up."

Whitey Hahn took a deep breath. He had never in his life crawled to any man. His life was his pride and had been through many rough years. But a time came when pride and life were lost and only survival mattered.

He threw the rifle aside and, so that there could be no mistake, unbuckled the heavy gun belt and dropped it into the grit. Then with his hands upstretched he walked slowly, painfully toward Pierson.

He heard Pierson's men closing in behind him, cutting off any retreat, but he had seen no opportunity for retreat since his horse had fallen. He even managed a kind of smile, trying to match the grin on Pierson's face.

"What's all the shooting about?" he asked.

"We're taking over the ranch."

"Alban's dead?"

"That's right."

"So take it over. It's nothing to me."

Pierson said deliberately: "We mean to." He drew his gun. He did not hurry. He watched the horror and regret spread like a mask, distorting Hahn's face. He drove two bullets into Hahn's naked chest.

Whitey Hahn fell down, his outstretched fingers closing convulsively on the grass. He gasped twice. Then blood rushed from his mouth and he lay still.

Pierson gave him no second look. He wheeled his horse. Hahn's animal had struggled up and stood on three legs. It was trembling with pain, and Pierson's compassion went out to it and he raised his gun and put a bullet through its head.

"Couple of you bury him." He spoke to Cap Norton, gestured at Hahn without looking at the dead man. "The rest of us will ride out and round up as many of the crew as we can, drift them out." Without waiting for Norton's answer, he signaled his men and took the trail.

The ranch office was in town but the working headquarters was a collection of adobe buildings and pole corrals some two miles out. Here were the bunkhouses, blacksmith shop, the grub shack, and a fenced pasture where the remuda was held.

A dozen of Whitey Hahn's men watched warily as Pierson rode into the hard-baked square. They were armed. Their guns hung ready. Their faces were sullen. It was obvious that they had heard of the violence in Gunlock and did not know where the situation now stood.

Gabe Pierson reined in and sat looking them over. They were men he understood—hardcases all.

"You know Alban's dead, I see," he said flatly. "I'm here to tell you Hahn's dead, too."

Their response was silence. No one moved, the ready guns were a defense, not a threat. He saw that none of these men meant to make any effort to avenge either of their bosses. Their interest was in saving and rearranging the rest of their lives. And this was the way Pierson wanted it. He wanted no one running to the authorities with a report, yet he intended no mass slaughter.

He said: "We're taking the cattle off the ranch. We're going to ship them, and we could use help. You boys know the territory and where most of the animals are. I've got twenty-five men. I can use a dozen more. Throw in with us. We'll sell the herd and split the take in forty shares. Everybody gets a share. Cap Norton and I will split the rest. You'll have more money than you ever expected."

"And if we don't?" The question came from a sandy-haired man with a weak chin and close-set eyes.

Gabe smiled at him. "What do you think?"

"How do we know you'll keep your word once we get them to the railroad?"

"Talk to my men. They know. There's no sense my stirring up trouble by double-crossing anybody."

The sandy man looked around him. "I'm in. No need to talk more."

The words were a signal for a chorus of unanimous assent.

Pierson picked up more recruits as others of the crew, who had been on the range, came in. Altogether, he had more than enough to handle the 10,000 head of cattle he expected to appropriate.

That night there was a celebration in Gunlock in keeping with the coup. Forty men rode into town as the sun dropped red in the west. The fifty-odd natives remaining in town, after the *vaqueros* had been run off, heard the pound of hoofs on the trail, the whoops, and read the message. They scurried to hide, but hiding was not the protection they hoped.

Bruce Alban had controlled the liquor of the community. Dobson, storekeeper and bookkeeper for the ranch, watched the invasion with failing heart. The afternoon had been a nightmare. It was Dobson who had climbed the hill to the big house and notified Virginia Alban of her husband's death. Virginia Alban, in her early forties, was still a good-looking woman. Nearly twenty years younger than her brother Mike Mulrooney had been, she completely lacked the common sense that had been his. Ray Dobson still shuddered at the hysterics his news had exploded.

He was a bachelor who knew little about women and cared less. He had immediately fled the house, leaving the widow to the ministrations of her two maids, less troubled by her grief than by the knowledge that, with Alban gone, there was no one to manage the great ranch. The idea had come as he returned to the store and looked across at

Alban's vacant office. If Virginia Alban decided to run the operation, she needed a new manager. Who knew more about the details of the ranch operation than the man who had kept the books?

That María would take over had not occurred to him. He had come after she had been sent away. He had heard and accepted the story of her simple-mindedness.

He idled behind the counter of his empty store, nursing and tasting the heady dream. He heard the pound of many horses and in quick fear knew that the outlaw gang was returning. He stayed where he was, held by indecision, hoping to be by-passed.

But they reined up out front—a roiling, dusty, noisy mob—left their horses at the rail, and crowded inside, laughing and joking among themselves about the completeness of their victory. They went behind the counter—Dobson scuttling out of their way, unnoticed—helping themselves to canned peaches, to whatever caught their fancy. Dobson stood at the rear, white-faced, afraid to utter a word of protest.

One of Whitey Hahn's riders had the inspiration. "Let's break out the whiskey."

"Where is it?"

"Back room."

They trailed back, jostling Dobson aside. They dragged out one of the kegs, and, because there was not room enough in the store, they carried it to the sidewalk and set it on the corner of the watering trough.

Pierson did not try to quiet the uproar. He was one of the first at the barrel, filling a tin cup to the brim, taking it down at one massive swallow.

A Hahn rider had an idea more to his taste. He moved down the street and stopped before the doorway, from which his late employer had bolted at the beginning of the chase, yelling at the top of his voice: "Chita! Chita! Come on out! Whitey's dead!" There was no answer, so he tried the heavy plank door. It was locked. Swearing, he retreated, then jumped forward, kicking the door with his foot. It still held.

His commotion attracted the attention of others on the street, and they came down, carrying their filled cups with them.

A Pierson hand asked: "Who's in there?"

"Whitey's girl. And she's something."

The man was already running back to the store. A moment later he returned with a borrowed axe, splintering the door with it until the lock broke. He tossed the axe aside, reached to take a cup of whiskey from one of his audience. He drank it and lunged through the opening. He reappeared, hauling a frightened woman after him.

She was small, with a round, pleasing face that showed only a trace of her Indian blood. She was sobbing, appealing to the crowding men.

They laughed. No one tried to help her.

Her captor held her by one hand around her slender wrist and ripped the blouse from her shoulders, the full skirt from her hips. She stood naked.

A shout echoed from the men around her. The crowd had grown. Nearly every rider had come running to the circle around the girl, yelling advice, laughing as she was thrown to the ground and her captor abused her. When he had finished with her, another man took his place. The girl had stopped crying and now made no sound. She lay inert, as if unconscious.

Soon one girl was not enough for the men. Other houses were broken into. Other women were dragged into the open and stripped. The whiskey barrel was emptied. Yelling men brought a second, kicked the first aside, and set the fresh one in its place. Months of repression, months of riding the lonely trails without sight of a woman had brought a starving. Insanity rode them as they sated themselves on alcohol and sex.

Gabe Pierson and Cap Norton took no part in the festivity. Norton had not touched the whiskey. Pierson held aloof to maintain his dominance over the men. Presently he turned away and trudged up the hill toward the big house.

Virginia Alban had heard the racket without attaching meaning to it. Her maids had deserted her when they saw Pierson coming toward the porch. They had bolted the door and fled.

Pierson did not hesitate at the lock. He strode to the nearest window, shattered the glass, loosened the catch, and swung the sash open. He stepped into the room.

The mistress of the house looked at him dully, saying in a toneless voice: "You have no right to be here."

He grinned. "I've got every right, honey. I'm the boss now."

He stalked her slowly, anticipating her outcry, expecting her to leap to her feet and make a game for him, trying to escape. She did not move. Even when he reached down and lifted her from the chair, she rose with no sign of comprehending what lay ahead. She did not react when he tore away her dress, her undergarments. She made no protest, no sound, no movement. She did not fight him in any way but lay as if she were dead.

She proved to be the worst experience Gabe Pierson had ever been through. But he had maintained his separation from the men. He had proved that he was king of Gunlock.

XIII

María and Dan Halliday rode from one *ranchita* to the next in the broken hills, growing more discouraged with each visit.

Mike Mulrooney's old riders were paralyzed with fear of Bruce Alban and Whitey Hahn. Some of them had been murdered. Some wives and daughters had been misused. And while the survivors nurtured a burning enmity, generations of taking orders had stifled their original initiative.

María argued, cajoled, pleaded. Fond of her as they were, they would not commit themselves to ride against Hahn and Pierson's outlaws. She wrung an agreement from each that he would ride, if the others did, but no one would take the lead. Ortega's lone voice was not enough.

María was bitter. "We've wasted a week and accomplished exactly nothing," she complained. "I'd have been better off staying with Pierson."

Halliday gave her small comfort. He was deep in his own troubles. The herd he had worked hard to accumulate was gone, so mixed with Gunlock cattle that he doubted he could ever round them up even if Bruce Alban permitted it. He considered killing Alban and discarded the idea. He would be bushwhacked by some of Hahn's crew. He needed luck on his side.

He and María returned to Ortega's small oasis nestling in its valley, and Halliday halted his horse, seeing the place as the end of trail for him.

"Well, what are you going to do now?" María asked.

He did not know the answer.

Pedro Ortega had preceded them home. Halliday and María rode down the slope to see him appear at the door with his gun, drop the weapon, and run toward them. He was calling something that they could not make out at once, his arms flailing in excitement. Halliday reached for his rifle, suspecting trouble. Then he caught the words.

"Alban *es muerto!* Hahn . . . *muerto*. They are dead, the both of them."

Halliday's eyes narrowed.

Pedro cried: "*Señor,* it is true! Juanita will tell you. Juanita came here this morning."

María slipped from her horse as Ortega's wife and the hotel maid ran from the house. She did not have to ask for the story. It poured out of the old woman in a hysterical re-counting of the night of horror.

"Every man was crazy drunk," she sobbed. "They dragged all of the women into the street and everybody used them. Only Dobson helped. He got a gun, but the Norton men shot him."

Halliday's tone was stony. "Where are Pierson's men now?"

"Driving the cattle to Bakersfield."

"How many?"

"All they could gather in a hurry. Most, I think."

"When did the drive start?"

"Almost a week ago."

164

"Why didn't you come for us sooner?"

"I didn't dare. I have been hiding in the hotel. The last man left only last night. I came then."

"All my cattle?" María said as if she could not believe her ears. "They took all the cattle? You're sure?"

Juanita lifted her shoulders in uncertainty. She knew only what the people of the town had said.

"Get me a fresh horse," Halliday said to Ortega.

María swung on him. "Where are you going?"

"Bakersfield."

"No. Whitey Hahn's crew is riding with Pierson's. What can you do?"

"I can see the cattle buyers. I can warn them that the herd is stolen, and that, no matter what kind of papers Pierson may forge, we'll hold them accountable for every head. There may not be any law worth the name in this section of the state, but we'll get a hearing in Sacramento."

"You haven't got a chance." The scorn in her voice was strong. She was blaming him for this latest turn of events as she had blamed him all along. "I should have kept my original deal with Pierson. I'd have something left."

Suddenly he felt that he did not care what she had. But he was not going to sit helpless and let Pierson and Norton walk off with his own herd—if only for his pride's sake. The decision gave him a lift. The thought of positive action was good after all the days of frustration. He felt freed. He knew that the job would not be easy. He knew Bakersfield had cattle buyers who would buy a stolen herd at a reduced price if they thought they could get away with it. There was no brand inspection in the state, and what little law existed in the area, the ranchers made for themselves.

Ortega led a rested horse out to the yard, and Halliday changed his saddle from his jaded mount. As he fastened the cinch, María came to him, her eyes wide, her breathing shallow with an unfamiliar dismay.

"Aren't you even going to say good bye?"

He did not look toward her as he said harshly: "I'll get you your herd. You see if you can scrabble together enough of your brave *vaqueros* to drive them back, after I settle with Pierson." He swung to the saddle, jerked the horse around, and drove it out of the yard at a full run.

María stood like a statue, watching him disappear. She did not believe he could succeed.

Ortega touched her arm. "There is nothing a woman can do to stop a man when he believes he is right," he said.

She jerked free angrily. "If you people up here had the courage of a fly, he would not be riding alone. There are better than a hundred of you, and you cower like dogs while one man fights for the only thing that can give you a livelihood." She mounted her horse. "I'm going to see if I can find one man left in this country to drive cattle . . . if not to fight."

"Wait. I go with you."

A newly determined Ortega ran for a saddle to throw on Halliday's tired horse.

Dan Halliday quartered across the country, trusting his sense of direction to bring him by the shortest way into Bakersfield. He had no food with him and he made a late camp beside the Santa Marguerita, not even bothering to light a fire. But although he had been in the saddle since early morning and it was nearing midnight, sleep would not come. He lay fully dressed, even to his boots, wrapped against the chill in the blanket that smelled strongly of the horse. He stared blindly at the arc of the summer sky turned milky by the myriad stars that hung there and some-times fell across it.

He was up before dawn and riding when the sun came over the rim of the shallow cañon. He kept a steady gait, not pressing the horse. The trail ahead was long.

Ahead, the land empty, the soil thin, the grass poor, but, as Halliday pressed on toward the lip of the big valley, the character of the terrain changed. The hills were lower, their slopes less steep. The grass thicker.

In the late afternoon he picked up a faint smudge in the lowlands, the dust cloud of a big herd. He watched it, marking time, judging from the rate of advance of the cloud that Pierson was pushing the animals strongly toward the railroad. He did not know how far he was from town. He made a guess, estimated the cattle would reach the shipping pens within two days. He began a wide circle that would bring him around and ahead of the travelers. The dust cloud stretched for miles. He covered nearly forty before it was behind him and he could cut across the herd's course. He rode steadily until he saw the winking glow of lights from Bakersfield far across the flat.

He rested briefly before riding into the main street and turning tiredly into the livery runway. The only light there was a lantern burning in the office. The old hostler slept in his chair, his head fallen to one side, stretching the wrinkles of his scrawny neck.

Halliday pushed open the office door. The rusty hinges squealed, but the hostler slept on. Halliday shook him awake. The heavy odor of whiskey filled the little room.

The man was drugged with liquor but finally got his eyes open. He asked sullenly: "What you want?"

"Who are the cattle buyers in town?"

"You wake me up for that?" The old man closed his eyes

and dropped back in the chair.

Halliday shook him again. "Come out of it or I'll dump you in the watering trough. Answer me."

The hostler did not open his eyes again, but muttered in a wheezing voice: "Lou Ziegler of Western Stockyards and Paul Nelson of United."

Halliday did not thank him. He went out of the building and stopped on the sidewalk, studying the street. It was a sorry place for the end of rail. The street, only four blocks long, ran from a wooden bridge and up the grade of the low rise on which the Fremont stood. At this hour it was nearly deserted. Only a handful of horses stood hipshot, heads down at the rails, while their owners lingered in the saloons.

Halliday walked the hill, pushed through the Fremont's split door, and paused to look around the bright room. Only one of the poker tables was occupied—six men around the green baize, under a hanging lamp. A few more were grouped around Kate Wormack at the end of the bar. None of her girls was present. They had either departed for the night or were entertaining customers elsewhere.

Kate saw Halliday and her face tightened noticeably. Two of her companions turned. Halliday grinned in spite of his weariness as he recalled the last time he had seen her. He walked toward her. She turned her back but watched him in the mirror.

He stopped. "Talk to you a minute, Kate?"

She did not turn. "Why?"

His eyes met hers in the mirror. "What are you afraid of?"

Kate Wormack stiffened her spine and came around. "Not afraid of you, Halliday," she said levelly.

He told the bartender—"Give me a bottle and a couple

of glasses."—picked them up, and moved to an unoccupied table.

Kate held back. Then with a defiant toss of her head, she followed him and took a facing chair. "I didn't expect you in town just now."

"You've got a lot of company in that."

Her brows rose. "Then you know Gabe's bringing in the Gunlock herd?"

"And mine, I judge."

She looked curious. "And you think you can take him on? How many men did you bring with you?"

"Me."

She laughed too loudly. "Just because you licked Gabe at my place . . . don't think you're seven feet tall. He's got more than thirty men with him, and they've all been promised a slice of the pie. Or do you think the law will back you up?"

"What about the law?"

"Tim George, the marshal . . . that's him, the big man playing poker . . . will tell you that he handles trouble in Bakersfield and no other place. The shipping pens are outside the town limits."

"The sheriff?"

Her grin was malicious. "An old drunk who hasn't made an arrest in three years. When he heard Gabe was headed this way, he and his two deputies headed for the north end of the county. They say they're hunting horse thieves. They won't be back until things are quiet here."

"Are you trying to warn me off?"

She studied him fully. "You're a pretty good man, Halliday, and there aren't too many around. You're sitting in a game with the cards stacked against you, like me. Gabe will bring those cows in and ship them, and then he'll blow for San Francisco or New Orleans and stay until he's broke."

"And you don't like that?"

She moved her round shoulders. "Men. I'm sick of men. Always going off to get yourselves killed. Why? What are you trying to prove?"

"I don't want to be robbed."

"Those steers aren't yours."

"Some are. The rest belong to my wife."

"Gabe told me about her. He said you abducted her and married her so she could claim her ranch."

"Something wrong in that?"

"I feel sorry for her. I feel sorry for any woman, and she seems to have had her share of tough luck. First her uncle locks her up in a mission. Then you come along and try to steal her ranch."

"Who told you I want to steal it?"

She shook her head, finished her drink, and poured another. "No one had to tell me. The story's always the same. Men use women. In this country no woman has a chance."

Halliday was remembering María's swiftly changing moods. "You want to tell me women don't use men?"

She gave him a level glance. Her lip lifted crookedly as she said: "We sure try. A few smart ones swing it. Not many."

"María is smart," he said quietly. "I understand a couple of cattle buyers are in town . . . Lou Ziegler and Paul Nelson."

She looked at him keenly. "You trying to scare them off?"

"When I find them."

"You'll have a time. Those boys are as tough in their way as Gabe is in his. This is a chance for them both to make a killing and they know it."

"It's a chance for them to get killed."

"Mister, you really do think you cast a long shadow, don't you? All right, it's your grave you're digging. I'll come to your funeral . . . and be about the only one in town there." She shifted her gaze. "The little man with the pointed nose . . . next to Tim George . . . is Paul Nelson. Ziegler was here earlier, but I think he went to bed." She chuckled. "And not alone. He went out of here with Martha."

"Which is her crib?"

"Third one back. But if you're figuring to break in on them, you'd better have your gun in your hand. Lou's short-fused and quick on the trigger . . . and he was more than a little drunk."

"I'll find out."

Halliday went into the night. He stood for minutes outside the saloon, accustoming his eyes to the dark. He went around the building to the row of adobe huts, paused before the third, and listened. No light showed from the cabin and no sound reached him through the solid door. His hand hesitated above the latch, then lifted it.

The room was black as a cave. A little light filtered through the dirty window and the open doorway only increased the gloom. Halliday stepped quickly in and to the side, taking his silhouette out of the dim rectangle. His boot struck a chair and crashed it over.

A startled shout rose through the blackness. "What the hell?"

"Ziegler," Halliday said, "I've got a message for you from Gabe Pierson."

A grudging mutter came.

Halliday risked striking a match. In its light he found the

lamp on the table, lit it, then looked at the bed.

A man lay there propped on one elbow. Halliday saw a heavy, bloated face and eyes puffed from alcoholic sleep. Beyond him a woman's black hair made a tangle on the pillow. Her gaze was vacuous with her sudden waking. She focused and recognized Halliday from his previous visit to the Fremont.

She swore at him, and said: "You've got a nerve, busting in here, Halliday."

"Halliday?" Ziegler's brain was still fogged with whiskey. "The Halliday that married Mike Mulrooney's girl? You ain't from Pierson. What is this?"

"End of the trail."

The big man was fumbling under his pillow for his gun.

Halliday said: "Don't." His gun came into his hand. The big man froze. "Now climb out of bed."

Ziegler glowered, on the point of refusing.

"I'd as soon kill you here as somewhere else. Get up," Halliday ordered.

Ziegler shoved back the covers and swung heavy, hairy legs over the edge of the bed, eased his feet to the floor. He was naked except for hair as thick as fur, and he was embarrassed. His embarrassment was to Halliday's advantage.

"Get dressed."

Ziegler rose and padded to where his clothes were dropped in a heap across a chair. He began to put them on.

Halliday moved to keep an eye on the girl as well as the man. She had sat up, exposed to the waist. Her breasts were large and pendulous. She drew back as Halliday came toward her, as he thrust his free hand beneath Ziegler's pillow and snagged out the gun. He shoved the weapon under his waistband and stepped back to watch Ziegler sullenly pull on his boots.

The girl said unexpectedly: "You owe me ten bucks."

"Go to hell," Ziegler snapped at her.

"Pay her," Halliday told him.

The man was just fastening his pants. He glared, pulled a crumpled bill from the pocket, and flung it toward the bed. He shrugged into his coat, growling: "Now what?"

"Walk down to the livery."

Fury shone in the puffy eyes, but Halliday's gun was steady. Ziegler walked out of the room and along the side wall of the Fremont to the street. No one was in sight. Their footfalls made hollow sounds on the sun-warped boards of the sidewalk. They reached the barn, and Ziegler turned in without being ordered. They passed the office door, and Halliday saw that the hostler again slept.

"Get your horse and saddle it," he told the cattle buyer.

Ziegler walked on to a rear stall, took the saddle down from the pegs, and put it on the horse, then led the animal into the runway, and stood waiting.

"You might make a killing, buying my wife's stock from Gabe Pierson at half price," Halliday said. "You might . . . if you got real lucky. But don't try it. You'll never ship a head of them from Bakersfield. If I see you in this town again, I'll kill you."

Hot intemperance blazed from the cattle buyer's eyes and his lips curled back from tobacco stained teeth. "You're a big man, holding a gun, mister. We'll see."

"I've ridden a long way and I'm tired," Halliday explained. "I don't mean to stand and argue. Don't come back."

Ziegler mounted, grunting, and rushed the horse from the barn into the night.

Halliday smiled grimly, guessing where he was headed, knowing Ziegler would ride directly to the herd. He would

173

report his expulsion to Gabe Pierson before the night was out. Halliday turned slowly back to the saloon, weighted down by the knowledge of what would follow.

If he knew Pierson—and he thought he had read the outlaw right—Pierson would come rushing into Bakersfield. Pierson would not bring the crew; his pride would not allow him to do that. Dan Halliday had licked him once, and the memory of the beating was still fresh. Pride would send him to shoot down the man who had defeated him, the only man who now stood in his way.

It was a sad gamble, but a sure one. It was also a safe bet that Pierson would make sure Halliday would not survive their next meeting, whether or not he beat Pierson a second time. What steps Pierson would take to accomplish that, Halliday could only guess at.

He stared at his gun as if he hated it before he dropped it into his holster.

XIV

The poker game still dragged on in the Fremont, but only two men remained beside the bar with Kate Wormack. She watched Halliday come in and studied his face as he moved to her.

"You're still alive." Her eyes went down and saw the gun thrust under the belt against his flat stomach. "That's Lou's gun." She looked up, her eyes questioning. "You didn't kill him. I didn't hear a shot."

"He figured to leave town." Halliday signaled the bartender for a drink.

The two men at the bar stood suddenly uneasy, sensing a tension they did not like in the situation. They glanced at each other, set their glasses quietly on the bar, and left the saloon.

Kate watched their reflections vanish in the backbar mirror. She said without rancor: "You're bad for trade."

He smiled thinly. "It will be worse before it gets better." He drank his drink and hung hunched on the bar, feeling all the weariness of the troubled days flowing through him.

The poker game was breaking up. The winners were cashing in their chips. Paul Nelson came to the bar for a last drink, smiling at Kate Wormack. The smile looped the thin lips but did not really touch them or his cool, hard eyes, or the muscles of his gambler's face.

"I'll be turning in," he said. "It'll be a busy day when the boys come in."

"A busy day," she echoed.

Halliday waited, keeping his patience, until the man had left. Then he slid his glass away, gave a studying look, then followed Nelson.

The cattle buyer was already halfway to the hotel. Halliday quickened his pace.

Nelson heard the rapid echoes of the steps and spun around, his hand dropping to his belted gun.

Halliday called: "A word with you!"

"Who are you?" The man's suspicion was sharply roused. He had won over $500 at the poker table, and his first reaction was that this could be a hold-up.

"Dan Halliday." He stopped ten feet short of his quarry, having no desire to kill the man unless he had to. But he was alert, ready in the half light of the stars.

The name apparently did not register with Nelson as it had with Ziegler. "What do you want with me?"

"To warn you not to buy the stolen herd Gabe Pierson's bringing in."

"And why is my business yours?"

"The cows belong to me, to my wife."

Nelson did not take his hand from the gun grip, but he did appear to relax and now seemed amused.

"Oh, so you're the character who conned Mike's daughter out of the mission."

"I am."

"And how do you propose to keep me from buying the herd?"

"If you do, we'll fight you clear to Sacramento."

Nelson laughed. "Have you any idea of the profit Ziegler and I will make on this deal? I won't be in Sacramento, friend. I'll take my stake and be on the first boat for South America. Wait until I tell Ziegler about you."

"I've already told him."

Interest tipped the man's head. "What did he say?"

"He left town."

"Probably went out to meet the herd. I think I'll do the same. I have an idea Gabe Pierson can handle anything you can throw at him."

"Maybe."

Behind Halliday a voice asked: "What's going on?"

Tim George's huge form came out of the darkness.

Halliday guessed that Kate Wormack had sent the marshal after him. He felt the pressure building on all sides.

"A friendly argument," Paul Nelson said. "Walk with me to the livery, Tim. I think I'll take a ride."

Halliday breathed from the bottom of his lungs as they turned away. Then he moved on to the hotel, his tiredness riding up through him in waves. He came into the narrow lobby lighted by the single lamp and hit the hand bell on the high desk four times before a sleepy clerk came from the rear, his nightshirt tucked into a pair of unbuttoned trousers.

"We're full."

"Which is Paul Nelson's room?"

The man looked at him, suddenly blinking.

"He won't be using it," Halliday assured him. "He rode out to meet the herd."

Everyone in Bakersfield knew about the herd. Halliday had assumed as much, and the clerk's expression confirmed his guess. Pierson would have sent an emissary to prepare prospective buyers for its approach. It would be the biggest shipment ever made from the local pens. The drovers would have more money to spend than had been seen in these parts in years. And the herd would have to be moved out fast.

"You from the trail drive?" the clerk asked.

"In a way," Halliday said. "Which is Nelson's room?"

The clerk took a key from its hook and tossed it to Halliday. "How many head coming in?"

"Maybe ten thousand."

The hotel man whistled. "Wish they was mine."

"Maybe you're lucky they aren't." Halliday followed him back along the hall. In Nelson's room he struck a match, lit the lamp on the bureau, and looked about. A whole row of suits hung from the rod in the wardrobe. He admired them, thinking that Paul Nelson was about as fancy a dresser as he had ever run into. But the bed interested him most. He stretched on it, not even taking off his boots. He was asleep before his head had settled into the pillow.

Tired as he was, he came awake as the early light came through the window. He pulled off his shirt and doused his face and head in the tepid water from the pitcher. The morning was already hot. He put the shirt on again and headed down the hall. The *clink* of crockery meant that the cook was already in the kitchen, and Halliday went into the dining room, ate tough steak and eggs, and washed them down with the bitterest coffee he could remember.

Afterward, he came out onto the street and looked along it to the wooden bridge across the river. People already stood on the sidewalks and the business places were opening. He found a barbershop and sank into a chair, relaxing, letting the man work on his three-month-long hair.

He traded a quarter for a towel and a bar of soap and

went into the rear yard. Here, curtained by a tattered piece of canvas, was a slatted wooden platform built on rockers above a sump. He stripped and stepped onto the platform, ignoring the curtain, putting his weight on one foot and then another, rocking the platform like a treadmill to work the pump that lifted water to a large overhead can with holes.

The morning sun had already warmed the water. He soaped to a thick lather, working the trail grime from his skin. He rinsed at length, his muscles giving up their tightness one by one until he stood loose, his body flexing smoothly. He toweled vigorously. He went to the store next door and bought a fresh shirt to replace his soiled one. The feel of the clean fabric made him remember the story he had heard somewhere of a gunfighter who always bathed and dressed with particular care before going out to get his man. That, he thought, was just what he was doing. He was waiting for Gabe Pierson to ride in.

And somehow the news of the coming meeting had seeped through the miserable town. Maybe Pierson himself had sent word—or maybe that sort of news drifted on the wind. However it had started, it had blown wide. As he left the store and turned toward the livery, covert glances followed him, conversations died as he approached.

Pierson would come to the livery. Halliday stopped outside the barn and walked a slow full circle like a general choosing a battle ground. Then he crossed the dusty road and stepped to the high sidewalk before a general store. A barrel sat on the sidewalk and he leaned against it, letting his body sag, supported partly by the barrel, partly by the building wall.

He waited. The sun climbed and brought the intense weight of the summer heat. A wagon with a woman and three children rattled without hurry into town and crawled down the empty road, raising a cloud of dust.

Then he saw Pierson far out on the flat trail. Pierson came alone.

He gave no outward sign of the new tension that coiled sharply within him. He still lounged against the barrel, a man with apparently nothing on his mind. But he turned his head idly, running his eyes along the street, alert for any sign of unexpected danger.

He saw Kate Wormack in the doorway of the Fremont. She was talking to Tim George on the street. He guessed that their talk was of him. He saw the farm woman and children come from a store and climb into the wagon and turn the team toward him. He cursed softly under his breath, afraid that in their slow passage they would still be within gun range when Pierson arrived.

But either because she had learned in the store what was gathering outside or because she was in a hurry to return home, the woman whipped up her horses. She took the light rig out of Bakersfield at a spanking run, leaving the dust to settle again like a slow breath.

Pierson was in no hurry—if the distant rider proved to be Gabe. Suddenly Halliday ceased to be sure. The rider remained a dot on the desert that seemed to grow no larger as the minutes dragged away. Yet he was moving. The dot did grow into a horse and man and finally the rider reached the outmost of the shacks that marked the western border of the town.

He was Pierson. He was deliberate, spinning out Halliday's wait as if by suspense he could stretch his opponent's nerves. He came at a walk, looking neither to right or left, but Halliday was certain Pierson had seen him.

Pierson turned in at the barn runway, gave his horse over

to the hostler, spoke to him, and then stepped outside. He walked to the edge of the sidewalk and halted there.

Halliday had straightened away from the wall. He no longer leaned against the barrel but stood in easy balance. They faced each other, separated by the broad bed of the street. They stood for a long minute, neither moving, neither speaking.

The pattern was familiar to both men, as stylized as a minuet, this formality developed by the men of the frontier to settle their differences, as rule-ridden as the duels of the early Victorian years. Halliday had sent his wordless challenge through Lou Ziegler, depending on Pierson's pride to bring him here alone. Pierson could have ridden in with thirty men and by their numbers overwhelmed him, but he had counted on the outlaw's pride to give him his only chance of stopping the pirating of María's herd. He had won the gamble.

"So you couldn't stay out of it." Pierson's voice came mocking and clear.

In the store behind him, Halliday heard the shifting of feet and knew that customers and clerks were hurrying out of the line of fire.

He said in the carrying quiet: "You didn't think I'd sit aside and let you take the cows, did you, Gabe?"

Gabe Pierson's grin was strong. "I figured you to be out in the hills and where you wouldn't hear about it until the critters were loaded on the cars. Better if you'd stayed out there. And you shouldn't have jumped Ziegler. You might have known he'd ride out and warn me."

"I did." Halliday was smiling. All his tension had vanished. All the frustration that had tormented him ever since his marriage was eased. This was his showdown. A man could face a showdown when he knew what was involved. It was the build-up that froze you. He said: "I know you pretty well, Gabe. I whipped you once, and you passed it off with a laugh. But you're not a man to stay whipped until you're dead. I've known for some time I'd have to kill you."

He was purposely goading the man. He wanted Pierson to go for his gun. He did not want to have to fight the marshal when this was over. He saw the telltale stiffening of Pierson's body. The half crouch. The hand had not started toward the belted gun, but it would. Soon.

"You'll never sell those steers, Gabe. You'll never collect from your cattle buyers. Think of it as you die."

Halliday saw the hand drop, the fingers claw at the gun. He stepped aside and drew. Pierson, his weapon already raised, fired too fast. The bullet cracked into the store front a futile three inches from Halliday's shoulder. Halliday fired calmly, unhurriedly, squeezing the trigger, seeing his shot take Gabe Pierson squarely in the chest. Pierson's gun exploded again, but he was already falling and already dead.

Halliday saw him go down without emotion, without even elation. He had believed in his ability to kill Pierson— as he had known he could bring Pierson to town alone. If you've whipped a man once, the odds are long that you'll whip him again. And the game had been fair. He had bet his life against Pierson's.

He stepped down from the walk and into the dust, his gun held loosely. And then it came—the shot from the barn across the street. The bullet caught the fleshy part of Halliday's shoulder and plowed a groove through the muscle.

He raised his weapon, but could see nothing in the barn entry. He turned and dove for the store doorway behind him, going flat as he slid across the rough boards, hearing the second shot strike somewhere above him. He screened himself with the door frame and peered across at the livery. He saw no movement in the yawning barn. He had not seen anyone enter the runway without coming out while he had waited for Pierson. But someone could have entered the livery through the rear without his knowledge.

His shoulder burned and the sleeve of his new shirt was bloody. He gave up his place and made for the rear of the store, keeping out of the range of the open door.

A horse was tethered at the loading dock. Halliday knew no scruple as he loosened the reins and mounted. His bad arm hampered him, but enough strength remained in the fingers to control the animal while he kept his gun in his good hand.

Whoever was in the livery was trying to kill him. He had to find out who and get him—or get out of town. From the street came the sound of voices. He rode his borrowed horse across the back lots, swung into a cross street, and drove up that. Curious eyes watched him pass, but he gave them no heed, spurring across the intersection of the main road and turning into the alley that ran behind the barn. Ahead, he saw the livery corral and beyond it a man bolting toward a horse tied against the fence.

The man was Cap Norton.

Norton heard Halliday coming, took time for a quick, startled look, then jerked the tie rope free and leaped to the saddle. He pounded down the alley, headed out of town.

Halliday followed, filled with a dull anger. He touched spurs to the horse. It settled into a steady run. He did not press too hard. He thought he probably had the advantage. Cap Norton had lately ridden in from the Pierson camp. The horse between Halliday's legs felt fresh.

Norton took the trail that led northwest toward the Gunlock herd. Halliday did not know how far out the camp was, guessed at ten or twelve miles. He meant to overtake Norton before he reached the herd. He shook up the horse and was gratified by its instant response. Half a mile farther he knew that he was gaining.

Norton realized it, too. He glanced back across his shoulder. Sunlight flashed quickly on his spurs as he raked his animal cruelly. But his best was not good enough. Halliday still gained. The distance between them shrunk to revolver range. Halliday did not waste effort on a chance shot. The odds of hitting a man with a short gun were long enough when you had both feet planted on solid ground. From the back of a running horse a shot at a moving target was folly.

Fear clouded Norton's judgment. He twisted and emptied his gun at his pursuer. None of the bullets came close to Halliday. Abruptly Norton swerved his mount out of the trail in a dash for a burst of broken rock thrusting up through the heavy brush of the level plain. Halliday angled to cut him off before he reached shelter, but misjudged the distance. Norton flung himself from the saddle, ran for the rocks, and vanished among them.

Halliday reined in and studied the lay of the place. For the moment Norton was securely hidden. Halliday was in the open. But Norton was afoot. His mount had already wandered away. Halliday kept out of short gun range.

Norton fired and a bullet kicked up dust in front of Halliday. He reined back and dropped from his saddle. He found an oversize fire bush, sat down in its small patch of shade, and took up his second wait of the day. Although he could not see his one-time partner, he knew that the man watched him, and at length the call came.

"Dan . . . Dan!"

"What is it?"

"Let's talk this over."

"What's to talk about?"

"Listen . . . you wanted the ranch. You've got it."

"I'll get the herd, too."

"I'll help you. There's thirty men with these cows, but they'll take orders from me. They'll turn around and trail back to Gunlock if I say so."

"I doubt it. They're already spending their share of the take. And they were Gabe's men, not yours."

Silence from the rocks. The sun beat on them and it was hot even in Halliday's bit of shade. He glanced at the sky and was surprised to find the sun already half down the western curve. Time had slipped away. He had not realized how long he had waited for Pierson. His shoulder had quit burning but felt as stiff as if it were in a cast. The blood on his sleeve had dried. He worked the fingers of his hand, thankful that they functioned properly.

"Dan!"

"What?"

There had been quiet for a half hour.

"I'll ride out. You'll never see me again. I'll pitch my gun over, and you can catch up my horse."

"Sorry."

"We were partners a long time."

"You should have remembered. I don't trust a man who shoots at me from ambush. You might have better luck next time."

"You won't kill me here in cold blood?"

"You can walk out any time. It's a fair shake. Just walk toward me. When you think you're close enough . . . start shooting. I'll do the same. Run and I'll hunt you down."

Silence fell once more. The afternoon heat climbed. Halliday knew that it must be murderous among the rocks.

Again he hated his gun—knowing he had to use it to kill deliberately—as he had hated it when he had set his trap for Gabe Pierson.

He wondered how much longer Cap could hold out.

Finally Norton's cracked voice said: "All right. If I'm going to cook, I may as well cook in hell." There was movement. Then Norton rose, his gun carried loosely.

Halliday stood up. He moved away from where his horse was tethered. Whichever of them survived would need the animal.

Norton saw the movement and stopped.

Halliday called: "No use killing a good horse! You never could shoot straight. Come on."

Norton stood as if he had changed his mind.

Halliday knew an impatience. He started toward Norton with slow, measured steps, gauging the distance at each step.

Norton was eager. He sent his first shot, and the bullet made a geyser of sand twenty feet in front of the advancing Halliday. The second struck him in the leg, jarring through the muscle without breaking the bone. He went down under the sudden impact, and Norton, too hurried, charged in.

Halliday fired twice. His second shot killed Cap Norton.

XV

The doctor was short, stout, and bald. He chewed tobacco as he worked, and Halliday guessed that he must swallow it. The office had no cuspidor.

The probe dug into the leg wound and the doctor grunted. "You got more luck than a square-head mule. Two nicks. Or maybe you just pick on bad shots."

"Maybe." The word came oddly through Halliday's clenched teeth. The probe hurt more than the bullet had.

"Quit making faces. A man who goes around getting shot up deserves all he gets."

The doctor cleaned the hole to his satisfaction, bandaged it, and went to work on the shoulder.

The door opened and Tim George came. He walked to the table where Halliday sat, and said without greeting: "Busy day for you. That was Bill Haycock's horse you took."

The doctor cut away the blood-encrusted shirt.

Halliday looked up at George. "He isn't hurt. I'll buy him. A good animal."

"Doubt he'd sell. Doubt he wants any truck with you. Aren't many in Bakersfield today looking for trouble with you."

"Thanks."

"But what do you see happening when that herd comes in?"

"Meaning?"

"I'm not going to have this town turned into a shooting gallery. I don't want thirty men hunting you down here."

"Neither do I."

"So ride out."

The doctor stopped working on the shoulder. "You're crazy, Tim. He's in no shape to ride. If you'd lost as much blood, you couldn't even walk."

"I'm just trying to save his skin."

Halliday asked: "Mind if I eat first?"

The marshal looked at him without liking. "Halliday, I've seen them tough . . . tougher than you. Eat and ride on. That's final. If you're here at midnight, I'll lock you up and keep you there until those steers are on the cars and the trail hands gone."

"All right. How about going and getting me another shirt? I'd hate to shock the girls at Kate's by going in there half dressed."

The marshal slammed the door.

The doctor shook with laughter, all 200 pounds of him. "Tim takes that badge seriously. Wonder he didn't run you in for shooting Gabe. I'll get you a shirt, if you give me the money." He finished with the shoulder and went on the errand of mercy.

Halliday rested, husbanding the minutes before he would need to be moving again. The doctor came back with a new shirt, and Halliday put it on. He had not bought that many clothes in a year before.

He went to the hotel and into the dining room. The twenty-odd people there stared openly. Conversation died. He ate alone, chewing the leathery meat and greasy fried potatoes, not because he was hungry but because he did not know when he would eat again.

He moved on to the Fremont. The room was well filled. Two poker tables were going and the bar was filled two deep. According to his way, he stopped just inside the door for a careful look, then went on toward Kate at her customary post. The girl who had been in bed with Ziegler sat with a clerk from the store where he had bought the first shirt that morning. He expected anger from her, but she smiled, instead. He winked at her and passed by.

Kate Wormack saw him in the mirror without turning. The men around her shifted away. She said when he stood beside her: "So you're proud of yourself."

He motioned to the bartender for a drink. "No. I did what had to be done. I suppose you hate me for shooting Gabe."

She twisted a shoulder. "If you hadn't shot him . . . someone else would have. He was marked for it. And a bullet's better than hanging. Who was the second man, the one you chased out of town?"

"Used to be my partner." He took his drink, slugged down a second, and filled the small glass a third time.

Kate turned to him, leaning her elbows on the bar. "Jumpy?"

He gave her a grin without humor. "Doctor said I lost a lot of blood. I'm trying to replace it."

"Replace it with booze and you won't be able to ride." She nodded toward the door as Tim George came in. "I hear you've got until midnight to be out of town."

George stopped at sight of Halliday, took a step toward him, then changed his mind and continued to a poker table.

Kate Wormack said: "George hates trouble because it means work. He was born lazy. And from where he stands, you spell all the trouble there is. You going to ride out?"

"Why not?"

"Thought you were going to keep your herd from being shipped."

"Maybe I changed my mind."

She considered him, shook her head. "No, you didn't. You've got something buzzing around under that flat hat just like you had last night when you sent Ziegler out to Gabe. That one worked. Maybe this one will."

He smiled and poured down the third drink. He left the saloon and walked to the livery. The arm the doctor had bound up bothered him and he asked the old hostler to throw the saddle onto his horse.

The old man sucked on his toothless gums as he worked, seeming highly amused. As Halliday lifted himself awkwardly into the saddle, he said: "Sure funny to watch them two fellows go for you this morning. Durn' fools. Gabe Pierson wouldn't listen to his friend that wanted him to pop you from in here. Said he had to prove to the town he was still boss. He proved it, all right. Now he's boss of a six foot hole in the ground."

Halliday looked down. "You seem pleased about it."

"Why wouldn't I be? The bastard was the meanest man on earth, used to kick the hell out of me every time he got drunk. I almost shot him myself several times."

Halliday used his good hand to bring a silver coin from his pocket. He flipped it to the old man and rode out, taking the trail toward Gunlock.

He did not know the time, but judged it to be after ten. That suited him. He did not want to hit the herd until the crew was well asleep. He doubted that he would find more than two night riders, perhaps three. He wondered who was running the bunch with both Pierson and Norton dead—

wondered if the camp had heard of the deaths, if someone from town had ridden out with the news?

He smelled dust in the air long before he reached the bed ground, long before he heard the soft talking of the resting animals and the toneless song of the circling men. He went in quietly, thinking of the ever-alert and suspicious steers. To cattle any strange sound had dark and ominous meaning, an inheritance come down through thousands of generations of animals nearly defenseless against every predator in history. And a trail herd was most vulnerable to panic. Steers driven through unfamiliar country find danger in every shadow, terror in every unexplained noise. They are keyed to run minute by minute.

The animals were bedded in a shallow depression rimmed on three sides by low, rolling mounds. On the crest of one of these, Halliday pulled up behind a clump of brush and had his look at the quiet scene. Nearly quiet. Here and there a cow was on its feet, bawling, keeping its fellows on edge.

Halliday's smile was thin. In the flat whiteness of the moonlight he could make out the movement of the riders slowly circling, singing monotonously in their continuing duty of keeping the animals assured that their dark fears were without foundation. He watched one pass below and later a second. He waited. A third man rode through the pale light—he judged the riders were equally spaced and represented the complete night detail. He gave the last man time, then drew his gun and raked his spurs across his horse's flanks.

The animal leaped forward and took the slope at a lunging run. Halliday emptied his gun at the distant sky and, through the thunder of its explosions, raised a yell— high, yipping—a screeching sound that split the night and had for its base rhythm the heavy pounding of horse's hoofs as it raced toward the herd.

In a writhing surge the big animals struggled to their feet. For a moment they stood confused, milling in indecision. Halliday used the moment to reload his gun. Again he discharged it, renewing the hysteria of his yelling.

The cattle saw the dark shape of the running horse bearing upon them. They turned away, and one, a little quicker than the others, charged off in the direction opposite to the threat, bumping through those in front of him. The stampede was started and its momentum quickened and spread. Nothing would stop the panicked herd until the frightened animals dropped with exhaustion.

Halliday was deep within the churning, horn-tossing wave, checking his horse, fighting to keep it from being carried along with the storm of cattle. A steer crashed into its flank and all but knocked it from its feet. It reared, pawing the air, until Halliday fought it under control, turning it, angling it through the tide until he and the animal were free of the herd.

The cattle would scatter over more than thirty miles. Weeks would be needed to round them up again. By that time the outlaws, without a leader, might spend their resolve, lose patience, and ride out in search of easier loot.

Now that the danger of his being trampled under the wicked hoofs was past, Halliday faced another. At his first shots the night riders on either side of him had wheeled toward him. As the herd rolled over the low rim of mounds— their former bedding ground—he was exposed. Reloading, he watched the two men charge him. Their guns flashed. He fired at once, at each, saw one veer away and the other's horse stumble and pitch its rider forward over its head.

The camp had come awake. Men raced for their horses

in an angry swarm, hoping to stem the stampede. Then, seeing that they were too late, they turned their attention to the flashes of Halliday's shooting.

Halliday spurred away. His way to Gunlock was blocked. He wheeled and headed for Bakersfield. He listened to the pursuit behind him and paced his own mount to keep his lead. He had more than ten miles to go. He did not want to run the animal into the ground.

A gun cracked, then a second, and a third. He saw that three riders were outdistancing the rest but that the sprinting pace they had set was beginning to tell on the leaders. The first two dropped back. A lone man on a rangy big roan continued to close the gap between himself and Halliday.

Halliday risked two shots, and saw the other check his horse. He let his horse out a little, drawing farther ahead but under no illusion that his pursuers would give up the chase. He had killed their dream of sudden wealth by scattering the cattle, and they would not be satisfied until they had made every effort to force him to pay with his life.

The miles stretched ahead. His horse could not stand the pace much longer, he thought, when, far across the flat plain, he caught the glint of the Bakersfield lights. Three miles. Then two, then one. His horse was staggering and pursuit was only half a mile behind.

The town lights threw a deceptively friendly promise— he remembered that Tim George had ordered him out. And even if the marshal were willing to stand with him, they would be two men against thirty. He reached the first out-flung buildings and swerved, coming up the alley behind the livery. He reined in at the corral and, without stopping to tether the horse, vaulted the fence, ran across the churned earth and into the barn.

The old hostler was asleep in the office and did not wake as Halliday ran through to the street entrance. There he paused, listening to the drum of the oncoming horses, now at the edge of town three blocks away. He ran the opposite way, keeping in the shadow of the wooden awnings over the sidewalk. Ahead of him was the Fremont. Across the street stood the hotel. The hotel was dark, but Kate's saloon was still open. He debated barging in on Kate for shelter, and discarded the idea. Others would be in the saloon, perhaps friends of the men now hounding him, and he was not at all certain how Kate Wormack herself would welcome him.

Better if no one in town knew he was there. The outlaw crew would find his horse, and the search would begin. He looked along the hitching rails. If he could find a fresh mount, he could ride out of town, possibly without being seen. But the rails were empty.

The hotel was out as a hideaway—it was one of the first places they would look for him. He thought of Kate's house, but noise behind him told him the riders were already in the side street. They would be coming up the main road in a matter of minutes.

He ran into the narrow passage between the Fremont and the structure next to it. The adobe walls were rough here, undressed mud bricks with grooves and hollows where they were imperfectly matched. The passage itself was barely two feet wide. By placing his back against one wall and feeling for chinks with the toes of his boots, he crabbed his way to the roof.

He lay, panting. The building had a false front. He stood up, climbed to peer over the top of it, and saw riders in the main street and heading for the saloon. They stopped below him, and he could hear their words.

"He can't have got out of town. He's got to be hiding."

In the shaft of light from the saloon window he recognized the speaker as the cattle buyer, Lou Ziegler, who seemed to have assumed command.

"We'll see if Kate's seen him, get a drink, and then look for him. I told Nelson and the men we left at the barn to start at the south end and work up. We'll work from the river. Go through every building, whether the owners like it or not."

They tramped into the saloon. Halliday squatted on the roof, resting, until the search was on. He wondered what they would do when they did not find him. He sat with his back to the false front, considering his next move.

Some thirty minutes later a voice hit him. "Here he is. On the Fremont roof."

Halliday looked across the street. A man stood framed in a second-story window of the hotel. Feet rushed along the street. He heard a chorus of excited shouts and muted, expectant laughter.

Halliday came to his feet, ran across the tiles toward the rear of the building. He was not fast enough. The man in the window shot at him. Pain seared his right shoulder and he was knocked to his knees. He stayed down, catching his breath while the high shout rang through the night.

"I got him! He's down!"

A second shot came. The bullet hummed past Halliday's ear. It spurred him to drag himself the small remaining space to the roof's edge. He fell rather than jumped, landed on his stomach. But necessity gave him the strength to drag himself erect. He stood before the row of one-room shacks behind the Fremont. Movement flickered ahead of him, and he drew his gun.

A white figure detached itself from the shadow of a wall. A naked girl ran to him, caught his wrist, and tugged, whispering urgently: "Come on."

He could not see who she was and did not care in his hurry to be out of sight. He ran with her. She hauled him into a cabin and shut the door quickly, quietly put her back to it for a moment, then jumped to catch him as he staggered. She pushed him toward the bed.

"Get down. Get under the bed."

Gratefully he sank to the floor. Then he heard a thick snore from the bed and hung back.

"What about him?"

"He's too drunk to know where he is. Hurry."

Halliday lay on his back and slithered under the low frame. The girl lighted a match, found a smear of blood he had left on the boards, caught a towel, and wiped up the blood, then tossed a throw rug over both towel and stain.

Halliday said: "Thanks. Why do you bother with me?"

Her voice was low. Her head was under the bed. Her words came matter of factly: "Return favor. You made Ziegler pay me last night. Nobody else in this lousy town has given me the time of day."

She crawled back on hands and knees and stood up, the pendulous breasts hanging, sagging hips white in the shaft of moonlight through the window. The bedspring creaked, and her bare legs disappeared as she slipped again onto the thin mattress beside the snoring man.

Halliday checked his gun. It held one bullet and his belt was empty.

Noise came from outside, the tramp of boots, the slam of doors, cries and shouts. A heavy fist struck against the girl's panel and her door sprang inward on squealing hinges. Lou Ziegler stood in the opening, a lantern held above his head.

Halliday heard the girl ask: "What the hell's the idea of busting in here this way? Can't you see I'm busy?"

Ziegler came to the bed. His boot toes were within inches of Halliday's face.

Of the man in the bed, he said in a tone of disappointment: "It ain't him." His feet turned toward the doorway. "Keep going. Try the next crib."

"Ain't who?" The girl asked. "Who did you expect to find, Santa Claus?"

The drunk chose this moment to awaken. He muttered: "What you doing here? This is inexcusable. Get out . . . of here."

Ziegler said in disgust: "Ah, shut up."

"I ain't shutting up." The drunk dragged himself to the edge of the mattress, and Halliday saw unsteady feet. "Nobody talks like that to Zeke Jarvis and gets away with it."

Ziegler evidently hit him, dumping him to the floor. Halliday found himself looking straight into the bleary eyes.

The man blinked. He shook his head. He peered, stretching his neck. He said accusingly: "What are you doing under the lady's bed? That ain't no way to act . . . spying under a lady's bed."

Ziegler had already reached the door on his way out. He stopped and came back. He dragged the drunk out of his way and leaned down. His gun was in his hand and he thrust it toward Halliday's nose. The disgust in his voice changed to deep pleasure.

"He's right, Halliday. Come out from under the lady's bed."

Halliday slithered out. He left his useless gun for the girl. Someday she might need one bullet.

Ziegler called two of his companions back, and, between them, they jerked Halliday upright. Ziegler motioned them to take him away, started to follow, then thought of something else. He turned and struck the girl hard across her face.

"That's for lying to me, Martha." He slammed the door behind him, leaving the crying girl with the drunk, asleep again on the floor.

XVI

Late as the hour was, Kate Wormack was busy behind the bar. The Fremont was doing a land-office business. The only idle employees were the girls who were ignored, shoved out of the way by the men, and huddling together at a rear table.

The men had trooped in, whooping with victory at having run a rabbit to earth and dug it from its hole. But now that they had Halliday, they did not know quite what to do with him. Nothing they could think of would gather the scattered herd or give them the golden reward on which they had counted. Any one of them might ride out, round up a few head of cows, and sell them—but the chore of digging 10,000 cattle out of the greasewood and pancake cactus did not seem worth the effort.

They drank to their success in catching Halliday and drank to drown their frustration. Singly and in groups they circled his chair, spitting on him, cursing him, mocking him.

They would have liked to tear him apart limb by limb, but a peculiar code restrained them. Bakersfield was their town. Tim George, the marshal, suffered them and their antics for as long as they made no trouble within the town limits. But instinctively they knew that any excess of violence would be considered an outrage sufficient to bring down government forces on them. Their sanctuary could be wiped out.

A lynching would have pleased most of the crew. Lou Ziegler argued for a greater formality. A trial would add pleasure to their vengeance, would draw out and add body and importance to an act that would otherwise be over too soon to be remembered with much satisfaction.

"We've got to try him!" he shouted. "Try him for murder! For two murders! He killed Gabe and he killed that new man, Norton!"

"In self-defense." Kate Wormack's voice was loud enough for its contempt to carry through the room.

Ziegler looked at her in surprise. He was more than a little drunk. Liquor slopped from the glass he waved at her. "I thought you were Gabe's woman?"

"I'm nobody's woman." Her tone lashed him. "Keep your tongue to yourself. Why don't you turn Halliday over to Tim George and go sleep it off?"

"I guess old Tim's gone to bed." Ziegler laughed, then frowned ferociously and weaved down the bar, shaking his spilling glass at the men strung along it to emphasize his points. "Besides murder, Halliday rooked us all out of more money than we'll ever see again. Is that right, or isn't it? How do you like it?"

"Hang him."

The words sounded like a curse from one man—became a chant. The rhythm took hold until, like Indians, the men began a stomping dance, snaking in a ring around their victim, giving vent to their chronic love of cruel horseplay.

"Not yet!" Ziegler was yelling above the chant. "Try him first. We'll hang him at dawn. You don't hang anybody in the middle of the night. You execute him at dawn. It's got to look legal as hell."

Dan Halliday sat in a chair at an empty poker table. His twice wounded shoulder throbbed. His leg ached to the groin. Waves of nausea rolled over him. Instinct made him fight against passing out.

Kate Wormack saw his head sink to his chest and jerk up again. She took a glass and picked up a bottle, carrying it by its neck so that she could use it as a weapon, if necessary. She weaved between the stomping dancers to Halliday's side.

"You look beat. You going to make it?"

His head tipped back unsteadily. He looked up blearily. He tried a grin and did not quite bring it off. "What difference does it make?" he muttered.

She poured whiskey into the glass, held his head to steady it, and lifted the glass to his lips, tipping the liquid into his mouth. He swallowed with difficulty. "I sent Josey for the doc and to find Tim George . . . told her to bring him here."

Ziegler had followed her. "I'll tell you where Tim is," he said. "He's locked up in his own cell. He tried to get in the way when we were hunting this bird." He snatched the glass from her hand and grabbed the bottle from the table. "Get away. Go on back behind the bar where you're needed."

Kate gave him a long stare. "Lice," she said, and went back through the circle.

Ziegler kicked out a chair at the hexagonal table, sat down grinning. He drank from the neck of the bottle and spewed a mouthful of liquor in Halliday's face. "Have a drink. Make you feel better? You were running high, wide, and handsome last night."

Halliday did not answer. He leaned the elbow of his

good arm on the table for support, rested his forehead in his hand, and closed his eyes.

Ziegler watched him with drunken gravity. "We're going to give you a trial," he said. "A real trial. And, as soon as it's light, we're going to hang you." He rose unsteadily, stood a moment longer above the nearly unconscious man. Then he swayed back to the bar, bumping through the crowd that had given up its dancing and returned to quench its thirst.

"All right now." He raised his voice. "Let's get started with the legalities." He stabbed a finger against Paul Nelson's chest. "You be the judge."

Nelson backed away in disgust. A fastidious man, he recoiled at being touched by anyone, particularly the pawing Ziegler. "You're drunk," Nelson hissed. "Be still and quit this foolishness."

"Gotta make it legal." Ziegler was too far gone to take offense. "Come on, judge, pick yourself a jury. Twelve men. Twelve good men and true." The effort of speaking seemed to sober him a little.

Nelson shrugged, not liking this brand of humor but knowing that his preferred method of disposing of Halliday would be considered by these men as cheating them of their fun. He would simply have walked up to Halliday and shot him in the head.

"Very well. From the end of the bar . . . the first twelve. You're the jury."

Ziegler straightened and strutted before them, tapping his shirt front. "I'm the witness against the defendant. You listen to me. That man there. . . ." He pointed toward Halliday. "Last night he got me out of bed with a gun and ran me out of Bakersfield. He deliberately tricked me into going out to the herd and telling Gabe he was here making

202

trouble. He knew Gabe would ride in alone. And Halliday shot him down in cold blood." He savored the sound of the words and said them again: "In cold blood, hear? And his partner that he'd had a ranch with . . . he chased him out to the desert and killed him, too. We don't know where he did it . . . but Norton's disappeared . . . and we can be sure he's dead. Now we've got to give the accused his chance." He turned his back to the jury and shook an arm at Halliday. "What have you got to say for yourself?"

Halliday did not even hear him.

Ziegler waited, then swung back to the bar. "The accused don't make any defense. Jury can now say he's guilty."

A happy jury announced: "Guilty as hell!"

Ziegler nodded his satisfaction and went to the front windows to look out at the lightening sky. "Joe, you go on down to the livery and bring a buckboard and a rope."

A man turned out of the saloon at a high lope, passing the doctor on his way in. An interested silence fell on the room and through it came the soft sound of crying from the girls' rear table.

The doctor's eyes found Halliday and he started toward him, but Ziegler stepped in front of him.

"Don't waste your time, Doc. We're going to hang him in just a minute."

The doctor's face was cold. "If you do, I'll see every one of you at the end of a rope."

A shout of laughter shook the room.

"You and who else? Who's going to do it, Doc? The sheriff or Tim George?"

The doctor stepped around Ziegler and faced Halliday. "You conscious?"

Halliday managed enough effort to speak. "I'm awake."

"Want me to take care of those wounds?"

"Don't bother."

The doctor weighed the worth of treating him anyway, then shrugged and walked to the bar where Kate Wormack stood, her face white.

"Hell of a thing," she said.

The doctor shrugged again. "From the looks of him, it doesn't matter much. Chances are he wouldn't last through the day anyhow. Gimme a drink."

She served him. "Maybe it's time this end of the valley had clean-up," she suggested. "Maybe we should elect a different sheriff."

The doctor gave her a sour smile, and asked: "Who's going to do the voting?"

The man who had gone to the livery came back in. "Rig's outside. All aboard. Bring him along."

Two of the recent jurymen caught Halliday under his arms. They dragged him through the door, lugged him across the sidewalk, and boosted him like a limp, heavy sack to the buckboard seat. One held him there while Joe, who had brought the rig, scrambled up and took the reins. The dry wagon wheels creaked and the buckboard moved down the main street toward the river.

On the bank beside the bridge grew one of the largest live oaks in the country. Its spreading limbs thrust across the roadway. One thick branch had been cut back, leaving a stump eight feet long protruding from the giant trunk. The tree was known locally as the hanging oak, and the bark of the sawed-off limb was scarred with marks of earlier ropes.

The driver took the buckboard out of the highway and under the limb. He stood up and looped the rope over it, then fashioned a hangman's noose in the end.

Halliday was aware of what was being done, but he did

not care. He felt no fear. He did not even feel regret. A man lived, did the best he could, died. He had at least delayed the selling of the Gunlock cattle. What could be done about returning them to their range was up to María now. He could do no more.

He heard the low clamor around him as the crew came up on foot. He heard women's voices and knew that even the girls from the Fremont had followed the party. He felt the rough hemp against his neck as the noose was dropped over his head and adjusted. He made no sound, no move. And then his eyes slitted open. It was all he could manage.

There was a new racket. Horses were racing up the street. He heard shouts, an explosion of guns. Halliday glimpsed a large party of horsemen charging down from the direction of the town. He was too dulled to try to make sense of it.

For an instant the outlaws were too surprised to react. Then someone pulled a gun and fired at the galloping riders. He was too late. The hanging party was overrun. Mounted men were swinging their rifles as clubs, their animals rearing and pawing, sharp hoofs striking. Short guns barked the crowd into submission.

María Mulrooney Halliday looked every inch her father's daughter at the head of the charge. She forced her horse through, careless about running men down, and wheeled at the side of the buckboard. She leaped from her saddle into the wagon, snatching the rope.

Halliday would have tumbled out of the cart, but María caught him and supported him on the seat.

The horsemen, better than a hundred of them milling through the panic, herded the lynchers like cattle. They hazed them into a tight group against the riverbank and, under Pedro Ortega's command, disarmed them.

They were not gentle. Too many of the *vaqueros* bore personal memories of the cruelty of the men who had lorded it over them since Mike Mulrooney's death. No plea for restraint from María would have protected Pierson's and Hahn's outlaws, and she made none.

The doctor had stood in brooding cynicism at the fringe of the mob until the *vaqueros* appeared. He weaved through the flailing hoofs and bludgeoning guns. He reached the buckboard. He shouted at María: "I'm a doctor! Get this man to my office . . . fast!"

One look at Halliday had shown her the need for haste. She caught the reins, whipped the team around, and drove while the doctor held Halliday.

Not until they were clear of the turmoil did she find breath to ask: "Will he live?"

The doctor looked at her sharply. "He's taken about as bad a beating as I've ever seen a man take. He's a crazy fool who doesn't know when to give up . . . when the odds are too much for him."

"It was my fault." Her voice was shrill with bitterness directed at herself.

This same bitterness had translated itself into the driving force that had roused the hill people at last. Under its lash, they had overcome their fears.

She sat now on the extreme edge of the hard seat, whipping the team on. She helped carry Halliday into the doctor's office.

Immediately he began to cut away the bloodied shirt, saying across his shoulder: "Get a fire going. Heat water. A lot of water."

She was doing as he had asked when Ortega came in. He asked: "What shall we do with the prisoners?"

María's eyes were on Halliday. "Whatever you want."

"Some of the men want to shoot them."

"Let your people judge among themselves. I don't care." She said it and was surprised. All during the ride to Bakersfield she had plotted the retribution she would deal out. Now the thought of revenge was meaningless. The only meaning for her was the life of the man on the table. She had needed to come close to losing him to realize how much he had meant to her. Abruptly she sensed she had put away her toys, become a woman.

Ortega left. She watched the doctor probe a bullet hole for the lead in the flesh. The forceps found the misshapen metal, worked it out. He held it up for her to see. She stared at it numbly. The thing looked too harmless to take man's life—to have nearly robbed her of Dan Halliday.

"How is he?"

The doctor was cautious. "You never know about a gunshot. He didn't die while I was digging, which is a wonder. And his pulse is strong for a man who's been through what he has. He's a healthy animal. There doesn't seem to be much internal bleeding. I'd be lying to you if I said his chances are good . . . but at least he's alive so far."

She spent the day beside the table, slept that night on the office couch.

She did not know that she slept until the doctor woke her in the morning. She waited anxiously as he examined his patient, his lips twisting into an expression she could not understand.

She asked: "What kind of smile is that?"

"His pulse may be a little stronger and his breathing isn't labored or shallow. A hopeful sign."

"Will he wake up soon?"

"Maybe in an hour, maybe in three days or so. No way to say."

She was begging for encouragement, reading into his words more than he intended—and decided that Halliday would recover. He had to recover. She would no longer doubt it.

The doctor read the optimism in her eyes and swore. "Get out of here," he told her. "You're doing no good mooning over him like a lovesick child. Go to the hotel and eat. Think of something else. Time enough to nurse him, when he knows you're here."

She met Ortega in the hotel lobby and smiled at him.

"The *patrón* will be all right." She sounded confident. "Collect the men and begin rounding up the herd and driving it back to the range. I want them all back by the time the *patrón* is well enough to come home."

He searched her face and believed her. "That is good word. He will understand our people. He will make the Gunlock great again, like your father did."

She felt an instant twinge of jealousy. In Ortega's eyes she was merely a woman and would never be more. Dan Halliday would be the real master of the ranch. She laughed aloud.

"I'm a fool," she told Ortega. "But from today on, I'll grow up fast."

She suffered two long, tormenting days of recurring uncertainty before Halliday opened his eyes. She was beside the bed, her hand on his forehead, when he did.

He looked up, not moving, his gaze steady yet doubtful on her. Then he closed his lids and she thought that he had lapsed again into unconsciousness until he said weakly: "The *vaqueros* do all right?"

"Yes. They're proud."

"Are they rounding up your herd?"

"Our herd," she said.

He opened his eyes again and stared at her through a long moment of silence. At last he said: "All right, María."

The doctor came in. "That's enough talk for now," he stated. "Clear out of here, María, and let him sleep."

She left, walking lightly in spite of her tiredness. She walked through the town and down to the river, and stopped on the bridge to see her reflection in the water. She looked down at the mirrored image and saw someone she had never seen before—a woman wearing the face of a child, yet ready to assume the responsibilities of womanhood. She did not care to be reminded of childhood or childishness. She dropped a pebble, watched the image shatter, and turned away.

Halliday slept through the afternoon and awoke again in the evening. On the doctor's orders, María fed him a little thin soup. Then they moved him to the big bed in the rear room. It was two full weeks before he could sit up, another two before he was on his feet.

They rode the buckboard to the ranch. María drove without hurry, trying to spare him the heavy jolting on the rough road. They climbed the first lifting hills and she halted on the crest. They looked down over the valley, along the curving street of Gunlock to the plaza and beyond.

The big house at the head of the street stood empty, waiting.

She told him: "Let's build a new place farther up the hill, away from the town. One that's only ours."

He said cautiously: "If you want."

"I want. There are too many memories in the old house,

good and bad. I want to forget them all." He looked puzzled, so she said: "Only when I nearly lost you did I find out how important a team we are."

"Do you mean that?"

She dropped the lines and rummaged behind her in the buckboard. When she turned back to him, she held out a gun.

"Yours," she said. "One of the girls from the Fremont brought it to me just before we started out this morning. She gave me a message for you. She said she spent the one bullet in it when the *vaqueros* came to town. During the fighting. She put your last bullet into the man you would have wanted dead, she said. Would that have been Ziegler? He was found . . . shot just once. Through the heart."

Halliday took the gun. "It would have been Ziegler," he said.

She kissed him. "A woman like that . . . I'm glad I learned about you before she had to teach me."

They drove down the hill and into the street and through Gunlock. People appeared in doorways newly repaired. Faces pressed against the new windows. A cheer began and ran ahead of them, filled with laughter. Halliday lifted a hand—a greeting, a salute, a thanks. They had accepted him. They cheered him. The ranch was his. But more than that—this girl beside him was his, his wife, more beautiful at this moment than he had ever seen her.

TWO TONS OF GOLD

TODHUNTER BALLARD

The Bank of California in the 1860s is a powerful company that pays its mine workers very little and will not tolerate strikes, sending in vicious strikebreakers to beat down any opposition. When Major Mark Dorne's father is murdered by strikebreakers, he begins a one-man war against the bank, always leaving behind his calling card—a small silver coin. Now the Major is ready for his most daring attack yet, the theft of five million dollars in gold coins from the Bank of California, from under the noses of the Wells Fargo guards. But his enemies are aware of his plans and have devised a foolproof plan to stop this war once and for all!